The C Hotel

Historical Fiction by

C. L. Swinney

Resources:

The Los Angeles Times.

The New York Times.

USA Today.

CBS Los Angeles.

Los Angeles County Records Office.

Los Angeles County Sheriff's Office.

Los Angeles Police Department, Central Division.

Authors James T. Bartlett, Leah Myette, Denise Hamilton, and Kathy Tran.

Los Angeles County Department of Medical Examiner-Coroner.

LACounty.com

KRON4 News

American Horror Story

Rick Jackson, Retired LAPD.

Paul Tippin, Retired LAPD.

Leroy Orozco, Retired LAPD.

Dora the Dispatcher, LAPD.

Acknowledgements:

I'd like to thank Rick Jackson, Paul Tippin, and Leroy Orozco for helping me with this project. I called them out of the blue and they stepped up big time. It's that kind of helpful spirit that I love about law enforcement.

A grateful thank you to the staff of Stay on Main (formerly Cecil Hotel) for their hospitality and allowing me to poke around the historical landmark.

I'd like to thank my friends and family for always supporting me. Thank you Joe for connecting me to Rick and pushing me to continue to write.

Lastly, I'd like to thank Dora the Dispatcher for suggesting this project. I had hit a writer's block for projects and never heard of the Cecil Hotel until she brought it up. Thank you, Dora.

Table of Contents

Prologue:

The Cecil Hotel, located at 640 South Main Street, Los Angeles, CA is an aberration. At conception, it gained significant appeal as affluent customers filled luxurious rooms, but the good times would not last. Shortly after opening day, the benign structure, and what occurred within its walls (and sometimes on the street or nearby building tops), began baffling police, staff, and patrons. Paranormal researchers and the friends and families of victims who passed away within (or leaping from) the hotel have often wondered if the place is haunted. Today, the building sits awaiting yet another face-lift or name change as recent investors hope to bring back the opulence the historical landmark had when it opened in 1927. Anyone familiar with the Cecil knows money and a name change aren't enough to affect the vibe and unexplainable situations that have happened at the hotel. Yet somehow, through the ups and downs, even after finding itself in the heart of Los Angeles' Skid Row, the Cecil Hotel always survives. Unfortunately, many people who've stayed there have not.

Hotelier William Banks Hanner in conjunction with W.W. Paden and Associates funded the Cecil Hotel project with close to one million dollars in 1924 (equivalent to over 15 million dollars today). Hanner's vision, along with that of architect Loy Lester Smith, included a 700-room Beaux Arts-style hotel meant for social elites, businessmen, and tourists. Once complete, the historic benchmark captured one's sense of sight, touch, and smell. A full marble lobby and massive grand terra cotta entryway rivaled that of the Titanic's Grand Ballroom, lavish stained-glass windows drew in various colorful rays of sunlight dancing off pristine floors, palm trees adorned the entire property while exotic plants filled the hallways with pleasant aromas, and a substantial staircase lead to beautiful Barker Brothers-furnished rooms upstairs. Barker Brothers was a major Los Angeles-based retailer of furniture, home furnishings, and housewares from 1880 to 1992. Without a doubt, the Cecil Hotel set out to impress everyone.

The one-million-dollar investment went far in the 1920's. No expense would be overlooked during construction. Rooms with a shared bath cost $1.50 a night, a room with a private toilet cost $2.00 a night, and a room with a private bathroom cost $2.50 a night. At the time, the significant design flaw pertaining to the bathroom design did not catch the eye of Hanner or Smith. That every room did not have its own bathroom proved extremely problematic because people didn't like to wait to use shared restrooms and they paid a high cost for a room and therefore felt almost entitled to have their own bathroom. Nevertheless, the building had already been built and gone over budget, so the restroom configurations remained the same despite complaints. The design flaw would be the least of investors' concerns as odd things began happening in and around the hotel -most of which were unexplainable. A certain cryptic mood surrounding the hotel began drawing the curious.

Downtown Los Angeles in the 1920's bustled as a wave of similar high-end hotels popped up in the central district. Businesses and homes trickled in bringing along a city infrastructure of schools, parks, a hospital, restaurants, and city buildings. Roadways began to take shape and the Grand Central Airport in Glendale led the charge connecting the world to Los Angeles. Although the Cecil project proceeded relatively quickly, it would be three years before opening day. Investors, hotel staff, and local law enforcement learned quickly that even the best laid plans can fall short -although the Cecil's fallen times would come a little later. In the beginning, times were great, rooms were full, people had fun and thoroughly enjoyed their stay.

Officially, opening day occurred December 20, 1927. Mr. Hanner and his investors wore wry smiles as their futuristic vision had finally become reality. Tourists, businessmen, and

Hollywood's elite attended the ceremony. Mary Pickford and Gloria Swanson wore elegant gowns while John Barrymore donned a clean tuxedo. Those in attendance lamented on the beauty, the grandness, and the ambiance exuding throughout the property. Within months, almost a year to the date, Hanner's hotel had become a focal point of the entire Los Angeles area. People flocked there to be a part of the one-of-a-kind experience. On the surface, the costly investment appeared sound. Yet dark secrets were buried deep within the foundation and one by one, something began exposing them…the story within the story if you will. Adding to the mystery, and the demise of the Cecil, would be an event that no one in the United States could have completely foreseen.

The US stock market crashed as a record 12.9 million shares were traded on October 24, 1929, igniting the Great Depression. As the economic downtrodden ripple marched across the United States, it found its way to California crushing Los Angeles -and scooped up places like the Cecil Hotel literally overnight. Five days later, panic-stricken investors sold another 16 million shares further plummeting the US economy to an all-time low. Unless you were quite wealthy (and depending on where one's wealth came from), everything people had ever worked for slipped away and no one could do anything about it. Jobs disappeared, businesses closed by the hundreds, productivity dipped, and wages dropped. Bleak didn't even remotely describe the situation accurately.

President Hoover urged Americans to "remain calm" and assured them the economic crisis would be short-lived. However, by 1930, roughly four million Americans were unemployed -the number grew to six million by 1931. That number represented more than 20-percent of the entire US population at that time. As a result, the productivity for the United States dropped by half. Soup kitchens, bread lines, and soaring populations of homeless people cluttered streets country-wide. Crops became too expensive to harvest and were left rotting in fields while people were starving across the US.

Further exasperating the drama were severe Southern Plains droughts coupled with high winds and dust through Nebraska and Texas -killing crops, livestock, and people. Steinbeck certainly had no shortage of real-life tragedy and drama for *Of Mice and Men* and *The Grapes of Wrath*.

And yet somehow things got worse. In the fall of 1930, the first of four banking panics ensued while hordes of investors lost confidence in banks and demanded deposits in cash. Banks were forced to liquidate loans to pay off debt. This trend carried throughout 1931, 1932, and 1933 -at which point thousands of banks became defunct and shut their doors. President Hoover attempted to support the remaining banks with government loans. He'd hoped they'd use the money to loan to businesses, who could then hire back their employees. It didn't work. Several years would pass and a new President would be elected before things began to slowly turn around. The Great Depression struck the Cecil Hotel extremely hard because people couldn't afford the high room prices and the landscape and community around the hotel became crime-

laden. The hotel continues to struggle today, even resorting to a

name change hoping to dodge a horrific past…Even though the

Great Depression occurred almost ninety-years ago.

Chapter One:

January 01, 2013. Peter Taylor floored the gas pedal spinning the rear tires of the BMW M3 he'd just stolen from Joe's Auto Parks at W 17th Street and S Grand Avenue, downtown Los Angeles. A life-long criminal with a need for adrenaline rushes, he waited until he saw a marked LAPD unit hoping to lead the cops on a high-speed chase. After that he'd dump the car and lay low at his room at the Cecil Hotel. As planned, the call went out, Dora the dispatcher calmly directed units to the in-progress crime, and Peter allowed a unit to get behind him before taking off like a shot. Expertly dodging cars, he sped northbound on South Grand, blew a light, and made a hard left to go eastbound on West Washington Boulevard. His father, his father's father, and his older brother had taught him to drive. Their family could best be described as notorious, and his role in their criminal enterprise had always been that of a driver… and paid assassin. He'd committed crime most of his adult life, and he knew cars more than he knew himself. Panic in the voices of the trailing cops blaring over his hand-held scanner produced a grin across his face. *These kids have no idea who they're chasing. Shouldn't be too long until the bird is up.*

More units joined the pursuit fueling Peter's insatiable itch to flee. The commotion of the air unit tracking him forced him to put on a seat belt. *Things are about to get real.* He made a quick left-hand U-turn to go north on Maple Avenue using the lanes of Interstate 10 to temporarily block the helicopter's view. He'd staged another car underneath the 10 and 110 interchange just in case he needed an out. The chase continued, but he made sure to stay within a few blocks of the Cecil just in case he got boxed in or one of the officers deployed a spike strip in front of him. Getting caught would not be an option. The last time he did prison time, he promised himself, and his daughter Ashley, that he would never go back. He did not; however, know how to give up a life of crime.

Thoughts of Ashley flooded his mind as the chase intensified. Near as he could tell, at least three cars were trailing and several more were setting up in choke points trying to keep him in a perimeter. *I need to move toward the hotel soon.* Suddenly, the service engine soon light illuminated, and he felt a rod go in the motor. *Son-of-a-bitch.* Police cars gained ground as seven or eight blocks separate him and the Cecil. *Time to ditch this ride and bug out.* He knew of an alley way off West Pico Boulevard near the Wren Apartments. He looked up, saw the police helicopter then read the skyline looking for the Wren Apartments marquee. *There!* The BMW sputtered as he slammed the gas pedal and dropped the step-tronic paddles to reach third gear. He didn't have much time until the motor let loose. The super-charged V8 allowed him to separate quickly from the police cars. He used pedestrians as cover, the sidewalk as his road, and barreled toward the split in South Olive Street.

White smoke began billowing from the front of the car as he spun around the median at South Olive Street and West Pico. Oil spewed from underneath covering the road making it slippery. The first three patrol cars through the oil lost control and stacked up blocking the roadway. Peter dumped the car near the back side of the apartments and ran as fast as he could. Being in shape and training for moments such as these gave him the confidence that none of the officers could catch him on foot. His plan involved running north until making it to the Ross Dress-For-Less store to change his clothes before doubling back to the Cecil. Tall downtown buildings prevented the line of sight of the police air unit and the confusion on the scanner confirmed he'd dumped the car perfectly and had little to worry about.

Peter worked his way through the Orpheum, made it to the Ross, and calmly paid for a shirt and pair of pants. He'd tried them on already and wore them as he handed the cashier the tags. The sweat from the pursuit remained on his clothes in the changing room. According to the chatter on the scanner, the police had given up and returned to work -except the junior officer left waiting for the tow trucks for the car Peter destroyed and the three patrol cars that piled up in the pursuit.

Peter walked eastbound, made a stop at Cole's French Dip for a hot pastrami sandwich, then over to the Cecil. He used a rear entrance hoping to fool any would-be followers. Another trait his family had taught him to avoid capture.

He saw Sam Richards, the building's maintenance worker, appear to pop out of nowhere. They locked eyes and Sam seemed like he had seen a ghost. *What's he up to? Is there a door there?* Peter's interest had been piqued, but he played cool. Another trait his family had taught him.

"Hey Sam, what's up?"

Sam froze.

"Sam?"

Sam stuttered, "Do I-I-I know you?"

They'd met up two weeks ago when Peter's toilet stopped working. Their shared interest in cars had been part of the discussion. *I know he's older, but how does he not remember our talk? Plus, I've been living here for years?* "Yeah, I'm in room 409. The bad toilet. A few weeks ago?"

Sam lightened up a bit, "Oh yeah. I'm sorry, I forgot. I seem to be doing that a lot lately. Toilet still working?" *Calm down. Take a deep breath. I hope he didn't just see me come out of there.*

"It is. Thanks again," Peter answered still suspicious of the man's behavior. *Is he playing me or what? Maybe he's getting dementia?*

"Well that's good. If you need anything, please let me know," Sam replied, made a right turn, and walked quickly away. *Please, God, don't let him find out.*

What the hell was that about? "Okay, thanks Sam."

Peter waited a few minutes then walked down the hallway toward the elevators. As he walked by where he thought Sam would have been standing when he spotted him, he noticed no door. *What the hell?* He didn't stop to investigate further. Sam had come out from somewhere along the wall, but he couldn't see where when he walked by. *Shit, maybe I'm seeing things. Maybe I'm the one losing it?* The urge to investigate further went away but returned later.

Around 2 am, Peter made his way to the rear of the Cecil and the hallway where he and Sam crossed paths. He felt along the wall and like before, noticed no doors. He used a pen light to shine in spots looking for a crease or any sign of an anomaly. Nothing stuck out as he worked along the wall. *I must be wrong.* He fished out a cigarette, lit it, and inhaled. He blew out smoke wondering why he thought he saw Sam coming out of a wall with no doors. The smoke fluttered from his face then instead of lingering away, it came back at him. *What the hell?* He blew more smoke and it came back at him again. He faced the opposite wall where he thought Sam had exited and knew the only way smoke would come back toward him is if air he couldn't see blew toward him. *There're no doors here either.*

Using the pen light and working the area along the wall, helped

him to locate a seam. He blew smoke at the seam and the

smoke rushed back toward him. *There's something here. Sam*

old boy, what are you up to?

Fifteen minutes later, Peter had the outline of a door

traced out. The next problem he faced became gaining access.

Peter fished out his Bench Made pocket knife and worked the

seams more prying slightly as he went. He still couldn't get in.

He decided to re-examine the area the following day, made one

last pass with his pen light, and stopped dead in his tracks. He

saw that dust had been disturbed on a maintenance sign and

tapped it with his knife curious to what that meant. *This area is*

rarely used. Why would this sign be touched at all? The sign

had been affixed in the 50's when this portion of the hotel had

been expanded. He shined light and could see dust on the

bottom portion in the shape of four fingers. He flipped the sign

with the knife revealing a lock. *Sam, you sly devil. Why would someone go through so much trouble to hide a door? Now I get why he freaked out. I wonder what's behind the door?*

Peter fished out his pick-kit and worked on the lock. Within a few seconds, he felt the side pins align and heard a click indicating he'd defeated the lock. The door then opened enough for him to fit his hand. He pulled to open the door completely, looked down the hallway one last time, and let himself into the unknown.

He walked down a short corridor and heard a humming sound getting louder as he moved. The laundry area would be nearby based on Peter's estimation, but he'd studied all available blueprints for the hotel and knew for a fact that the spot had not been listed anywhere. His family, at least for three generations, had used the hotel as a safe-haven. It had become the focal point of their criminal activities, and no one knew except blood family members. He negotiated a few small turns and came to an area that opened considerably. He looked for a light, found a switch, and flipped it. Being discovered in the room hadn't crossed his mind, but what he saw as his eyes adjusted to the light caught him off-guard and caused him a bit of concern. *I don't have much time before I need to split. This is some insane shit right here.*

The room smelled musty and could be described best as dingy. A large worn brown wooden table sat in the middle of the room. On top of the table were books, encyclopedias, random stacks of paper and magazines, a small black computer, a stapler, a can wrapped with letters that spelled D-A-D, various colors of string, tape, and three pairs of scissors. Three walls were covered in photographs, newspaper clippings, signs, and Post-it notes. In the middle of all these items were large color posters of the Cecil Hotel from the day it opened in 1927. Strings connected photos to newspaper articles to the hotel and on the east wall a timeline that read "Cecil Horror" could be seen. *Oh my God, Sam's a psycho! What the hell is he doing in here?*

Gray cardboard boxes lined the bottom of the walls. Peter opened one and saw more newspaper articles and stacks of photographs. He dug through some of them and noticed most had headlines about death, suicide, or murder at the Cecil Hotel. He grabbed a stack intending to take them but grew concerned that Sam would eventually realize someone had been there if he did. He turned his attention to the walls again and snapped photos with his cellphone. His internal clock said he needed to leave soon. He could handle himself with Sam if he stumbled upon him, but he didn't want to hurt him. He had no beef with Sam and didn't like to hurt people if he didn't have to. Peter could be violent for the right price… or when boxed in a corner. After snapping a few more photos, he left the room as quietly as he came leaving no clue that he'd been inside. Or so he assumed.

After examining the photos, it became clear to Peter that the Cecil Hotel had many more terrible secrets than he, or his family, had any idea of. He could not look away from the photos and the strings, Post-it notes, and newspaper articles.

Something about them called to him. They painted a picture

even his criminal mind had a difficult time processing. Until

now, no one knew what Peter's pictures contained. This is

based on the photos in that room and the true events that

occurred at the Cecil Hotel from 1927 to present day.

Chapter Two:

November 13, 1931. Mr. James Willys entered the illustrious Cecil Hotel wide-eyed and curious. The new structure, well-adorned rooms, and the buzz of the place had caught his attention during a time when his mind often drifted. He paid to rent a room for one week and told the front desk he hailed from Chicago. According to police, none of the staff or other folks who frequented the hotel recalled anything astonishing or unique about Mr. Willys. He'd later be described as "non-descript, normal, like most" of the people found at the Cecil. Mr. Willys came and went without anyone noticing. He did not have a set routine. He did not return with any guests, and he had no known visitors. In fact, the less attention he garnered the better. James weighed his life's most difficult decision all day every day. Until the very end, good outdueled evil.

On November 19, 1931, a maid knocked on his door. Susan Johnson, on the job for a few months, received no response. She didn't smell anything odd and did not hear anything emanating from the room that would alert her to something possibly being wrong. Susan thought nothing of the non-response, fished the master-key from her dress, and let herself in. As she walked around the corner, she saw a male body, clothed, and sprawled out on the twin-bed. The sight caught her off-guard, but surprisingly she didn't panic. Susan quickly alerted the hotel manager, who phoned the police. They told the police nothing seemed "off or weird" in the room, besides the sight of the dead man on the bed. Susan hadn't seen a dead body before. Once the sight finally hit her, she quit. The sight of a dead body hits everyone differently. She'd be one of hundreds of people who would quit as the hotel brought them down and made them feel odd.

A quick preliminary assessment by police revealed no foul play or robbery. No weapons or drug paraphernalia were located. No suicide note would be found. As detectives searched the victim's body, they located several non-descript pills in a vest pocket; they assumed the pills were poison (there's no indication as to how they made such a quick conclusion). Unlike today, when folks use firearms and jumping more commonly for suicide, poison had been the means to end one's life in the early 1900's.

Three checks made out to "Mrs. M. C. Morton" were found in the victim's trouser pocket, leading police to believe the dead man likely had a different name. Although thieves and crime existed in the 1920's, something like identity theft or check fraud rarely, if ever, occurred.

As the victim was placed in the ambulance (despite being clearly deceased indicated through obvious "heavy" rigor mortis), detectives learned the victim's true name, W. K. Norton -aged 46 at the time of his death. Mr. Norton had been recently reported as missing from his home located at 912 Strand Avenue, Manhattan Beach -and obviously did not hail from Chicago. He'd used a fake address and name because he'd chosen to escape Manhattan Beach and did not want to be located. His mind had not been right since the Great Depression began. Hoping to avoid negative press for the hotel, the hotel manager requested the victim be transported off property - James Miller, always an astute manager, understood that it looked bad if someone committed suicide at the establishment.

Despite quick-thinking and intervention by Mr. Miller, word spread of the first known suicide occurring at the Cecil Hotel. Management had already lowered rates (although only slightly) to combat the significant dip in patronage due to the waning effects of the Great Depression. Word spread about the fact that every room did not have its own bathroom. As such, dissension swirled. The suicide of W. K. Norton certainly did not help matters.

Mr. Norton's incident is classified as "suicide" to this day, mostly because there's zero evidence of murder. In addition, the pills were later examined and officially labeled as "toxic." Police were able to locate his wife and advised her of his passing. Mrs. Norton told them her husband suffered from depression and their financial affairs weighed on him heavily. She would be distraught of the news of his passing, but when he disappeared, she knew it would only be a matter of time before he ended up dead. Depression and money problems are among the highest reasons why people take their own lives, even today.

On cue and in line with Mr. Norton's passing, the streets and structures near the hotel, once bustling and refreshing, slowly began to turn into make-shift homeless shelters, drug abuse grew exponentially, and violence erupted. The vision of what the Cecil Hotel could have been, and had been on its way to becoming, slipped away. Likewise, many of the hotels and businesses in the area would file for bankruptcy. The Cecil would endure, but at a tremendous cost.

The passing of Mr. Norton did not signify the first significant black eye for the property, although most historians cite his incident as the beginning. On April 17, 1929, a woman had been spotted walking around the hotel and property who seemed a bit "off." Apparently, she'd been meandering for three days before someone took notice. She had a Cecil room key but didn't seem completely together. Her initial behavior seemed irrelevant until *after* she caused a crazy scene.

On day three, Mrs. Dorothy Roberson, aged 33, collapsed near the main stairway in the lobby amidst numerous people. Gasps and shock fluttered about the room, yet no one ran to the woman's side. Likewise, no one began providing her aid. Some believed Mrs. Roberson died on the floor; however, she'd be transported to the hospital and survived with quick medical attention. Unfortunately, she didn't want to be alive and tried to end things on her own.

A hospital social worker noted that Mrs. Roberson had taken a large amount of barbiturates. The unexplainable and sudden passing of her husband had become too much for her to bear. Grief and depression would be sentiments found commonly among guests of the Cecil Hotel...strange since the

Cecil begged for positive attention. It turned out that the hotel attracted the very worst attention imaginable.

Since Mrs. Roberson did not pass away, no one talked about the incident for very long. Even in the 1920's, something needed to be sensational to remain on the minds of others for a long period of time. Merely transporting a patron from the grounds wouldn't cause business to slow. That is true. Still, the incident served as the true beginning of horror to come. A certain negative aura had developed and took root. Whatever nastiness working in the background in the twenties has not left… and likely never will. And why would it? It has too much fun attracting murder and murderers.

———————

September 7, 1932. Less than a year after Mr. Norton's suicide, a maid once again let herself into a room to tidy up and made a gruesome discovery. A young white male adult, later identified as Benjamin Dodich, aged 25, lay sprawled out on the floor…his head rested in a pool of coagulated blood. Blood splatter, reminiscent of a scene on *Dexter*, covered the wall and ceiling near the bed. A small black revolver lay on the floor near the body. Nothing else seemed out of place. The maid did not poke around before going downstairs to contact James Miller who alerted the police while rolling his eyes. His day had already been bad, the news of a dead person in the hotel did not sit well with him.

Once on scene, the investigators processed evidence and searched for clues in case they'd stumbled upon a murder. A suicide note did not exist. No next of kin were available. The victim's wallet, found in his trouser pocket, still contained a small amount of cash. None of the victim's belongings appeared missing or riffled through. Everything in the room pointed toward suicide…therefore, the thought of the case having anything to do with murder never had traction.

Technology available to investigators today did not exist back then. Even though the detectives canvassed the hotel and the floor where the incident occurred (as well as above and below), no one reported hearing a gunshot blast. This caused suspicion since the building's walls were not thick and normally very little ambient noise could be found on the living floors of the Cecil. After careful consideration and scrutiny of the available evidence at the scene, the police confirmed the injury to be self-inflicted and ruled Mr. Dodich's death a suicide. The coroner report echoed the same conclusion: suicide.

Mr. Dodich's case furthered the negativity surrounding the community and hotel. How did a young handsome man end up killing himself at the Cecil Hotel? Where was his family? Who was he? What could have possibly been so terrible to cause him to end his life so abruptly? So many questions swirled around like the spirits in Disney's Haunted Mansion ride. Whatever Mr. Dodich's real story had been, it remained unfinished and incomplete…but his death served as his final chapter.

Chapter Three:

July 26, 1934. Mr. Louis D. Borden signed the guest registry at the front desk, grabbed his small leather bag containing clothing and toiletries, and let himself into his room on the fourth floor. Within his belongings were a pad of paper, two pencils, a razor, and several replacement razor blades. On the surface these items seem normal, but what Mr. Borden had intended to do with them turned out to be shocking. Like most guests, Mr. Borden did not present as extraordinary, just another face in the crowd. Like most of us, though, he held a troublesome secret tightly to his heart. It made him think life wasn't worth living anymore. A medical diagnosis of cancer is never easy to comprehend or accept, and certainly in 1934 the diagnosis would have been far bleaker. The cancer had made Mr. Borden a shell of his former physically-fit self...as a military man, he couldn't handle being frail.

The room smelled musty, albeit the bed had been made nicely and the sheets were clean. Ben Selvin's, *I only have eyes for you,* played softly in the background. Mr. Borden sat in the small room, alone and heartbroken. His entire adult life revolved around the military. It had given him a home when he had none, friends when he had none, and a strong sense of finally belonging to something. The military had become his family. Louis' life held meaning within the Army. Nevertheless, his mind raced with what to do next. With each minute that passed, his thoughts pushed him closer to his own death.

He retrieved a piece of paper and one of the pencils from his bag. Suddenly a mind full of thoughts and feelings went numb and no matter how hard he tried, he couldn't begin to write. The writing exercise became a desperate attempt to rationalize taking his own life. After a few hours, he finally found the courage to make words form with the pencil. The fact that him, nor the doctors, couldn't do anything about his ailing health pushed him into a bout of unbelievable depression. Having been a man of purpose and in control his entire life, he now found himself helpless with no control. He lost all will to stay alive.

As a medic in the Army Medical Corps, he knew precisely how to save a life; however, his training and experience also taught him ways he could take life. Before that moment, he never thought the life he would take would be his own. His schooling and profession drove him to save lives, not end them. The internal struggle, overwhelming and tormenting, consumed his every thought.

On July 27, 1934, retired Army Medical Corps Sgt. Louis D. Borden, aged 53, applied direct and firm pressure with a clean razor along his carotid artery and in a surgical manner cut himself causing a wound he knew would be fatal. He bled out quickly, slumped over, and ended up sprawled on the floor. Whatever demons he let win were finally set free. As a service man, and a good person, this manner of passing served him no justice. Duke Ellington's, *Cocktails For Two,* could be heard in the background as time moved on less one honest and good man.

One hour past checkout time, a seasoned maid named Linda, let herself into Mr. Borden's room. She immediately saw an older white male adult, pale in color, and a large amount of blood. The sight caused Linda to yelp and back out. She left the door ajar and contacted the head maid who quickly contacted the front desk. Once again, Mr. Miller rolled his eyes as he dialed for help. James began to wonder why people were coming to *his* hotel to commit suicide.

Police arrived and were led to Mr. Borden's room. Upon entry, the detectives noted no sign of struggle, a deceased male adult on the floor, and quite a bit of blood. Next to the man police located a full-length barber shop razor blade, also covered in blood. The coroner carefully laid the victim flat on his back, searched his pockets, and located an identification card. The photo on the card matched the victim and listed the name of Louis D. Borden. Another military identification matched the name and photo of the deceased.

On the brown and worn bedside table were several handwritten notes. One mentioned, "Please notify Mrs. Edna Hasoner of what has happened here. She should be the sole beneficiary of the little that I leave." Other notes listed Mrs. Hasoner's name and address (PO Box 664, Edmonds, Washington). Police attempted to contact Mrs. Hasoner, but their efforts came up empty. Louis and Edna were once lovers, but she chose to remain married and cut things off with Louis. She convinced her husband to move fearing Louis would return someday wanting more. Clearly, he never got over his feelings for her, but she did not feel the same. Sadly, his request to leave her something went unanswered. She'd done her best to forget him, but occasionally she thought about the two-week affair they had.

Like the suicide of Mr. Dodich, the incident with Mr. Borden brought more questions than answers. What compelled him to take his life specifically at the Cecil Hotel? The United States found itself smack dab in the middle of the Great Depression at the time. Rooms were not cheap, and Mr. Borden did not have much money, so why the Cecil? It's as if whatever sorcery that beckoned him wanted to see him take his own life and strengthen the very real stigmatism looming over the hotel. Some staff members and newspaper writers jokingly called the Cecil, "The Suicide." The name wouldn't stick, but it would come back in the late 50's and 60's as a reminder of how long things had been bad at the property.

March 4, 1937. Grace E. Margo paid for a room for three days. Her cantankerous attitude spilled over to anyone she spoke to. Life had been rough on her and she felt that meant everyone else should suffer. Even the light-yellow day dress she wore seemed angry. Grace refused to answer any of manager Miller's questions and demanded a room key. All sorts of people with a myriad of personalities consistently walked through the foyer, none of them impressed Mr. Miller. He took Ms. Margo's money, slid the room key to the bitter guest, and pointed to the stairs. She huffed and stormed off to her room mumbling obscenities under her breath.

The following morning, Grace ordered a clerk to locate Mr. Miller so she could file a complaint. The clerk pointed her toward his office and made an about-face slipping away to his other responsibilities.

After a few unanswered knocks, Grace started in, "Mr. Miller, I beg your pardon. I have a complaint." Various staff wandered by and shook their heads at Ms. Margo while she created a scene.

Mr. Miller tucked his light gray wool two-pocket sport shirt into his light brown pressed trousers as he opened his office door, "Yes, Ma'am, how can I be of service?" Secretly he loathed the woman, but to keep his job, he needed to make guests happy.

"The toilet down the hall isn't working! What kind of establishment are you running?" Grace snarled.

"I'm sorry madame," he turned and reached for his desk phone, "I'll send maintenance immediately."

"I'm stepping out for a bit. I trust it will be in working order when I return," before Mr. Miller could assure her the problem would be resolved she added, "Otherwise, I'll find another establishment." She turned and left before he could answer.

As promised, the toilet had been restored to working order. Ms. Margo returned, discovered the toilet running satisfactorily, but did not thank anyone. She did, however, take the time to walk around the Cecil looking for issues to point out to staff. By the end of the evening, she'd counted eleven more items that she demanded be fixed. To say no one, including other guests, cared for Grace became an understatement. In just over one day, she'd managed to turn an entire hotel against her -she could care less what anyone thought about her, though.

On March 6, Grace woke and attempted to open her window wider hoping to freshen the room. It stuck a little, and her blood pressure sky-rocketed, giving her a little more energy to force open the window as wide as it could open. As she looked outside, she hesitantly admitted that she enjoyed the view from the ninth floor. She allowed herself to get closer to the window but dare not look down being deathly afraid of heights. A gust of wind, or a wicked spirit, swirled around her, into her room, then pushed with unreal pressure from behind her. The force propelled Grace catching her off-guard causing her to stumble and lose her grip. Desperately, she reached for the window sides and curtains, but could not grab them. Within a flash, Grace plummeted toward the pavement.

As she fell, her body struck telephone wires, lessening the impact she made with the street below. Grace screamed in shock as she fell, causing pedestrians to look up and see the surreal sight. Her body smacked the ground despite being tangled in wires. The impact broke bones and knocked Grace unconscious, but it did not initially kill her. Police were called, as were an ambulance and firemen.

The sight of Ms. Margo wrapped in wires suspended in the air drew quite a spectacle outside the Cecil Hotel. Reporters were able to make it before firemen and other first responders could get her down. They worked quickly because the victim had a slight pulse and they could hear her wheezing. The ambulance took Grace to Georgia Street Receiving Hospital (which no longer exists).

As doctors struggled to keep Grace alive, police had a difficult time trying to determine what happened at the Cecil. Did she legitimately fall while looking outside or did she jump? As with other suspicious circumstances at the hotel, when police asked if anyone had seen or heard anything, everyone just replied, "No." I've investigated people committing suicide or attempting to commit suicide from buildings. They make very little sound when jumping; however, depending on what they strike, if anything, it can alert others to what just happened. In this case, Grace screamed at the top of her lungs as she descended, indicating more likely that she accidentally fell. The fact no one saw anything makes sense because no one would have been in her room. Outside, plenty of people saw her fall.

The following day, Grace passed away from the injuries she sustained. Word of her passing made it back to the Cecil. No one felt an ounce of remorse for the bitter woman. Mr. Miller immediately sent staff to clean and make her room ready for the next guest. Her belongings were thrown in the dumpster and forgotten. No next of kin were available.

The police report listed the incident as, "suspicious circumstance." Based on where Grace landed initially, the coroner theorized that she leaped to her death. The trajectory seemed more likely that she had a running start but running and negotiating the window space to then leap from the building would have required perfect timing and Grace contorting her body oddly to get through the window. This didn't seem to explain what happened. Some speculated that perhaps she'd been pushed hard from behind, which explained how she ended so far out and over the telephone lines. Although murder had been considered, investigators later ruled it out. Officially, it's not entirely clear to medical staff or law enforcement how exactly Grace managed to leap so far from the hotel. Whatever pushed her ended a lifetime of anger, depression, and consternation.

Some seventy-seven years later, (remember the number seven as this story unfolds) a bizarre report of a ghost sighting near a window at the Cecil surfaced in the news. Historical buffs and ghost chasers have suggested the ghost image is that of Grace E. Margo. The novelty of the alleged sighting wore off quickly and the story of Grace Margo ended as quickly as it had originally begun.

Grace's passing, natural or unnatural, began a string of three suicides, one each year, enshrouding the Cecil in uncertainty. This suspicion still plagues the establishment today.

Chapter Four:

January 2, 1938. Roy Thompson secured a room having no idea where each day, each moment even, would take him. Being charming and outgoing made it so staff enjoyed speaking to him. For the first six days, Roy interreacted with people and seemed upbeat. On day *seven*, mid-morning, Roy walked through the lobby and didn't say hello to anyone. His demeanor had completely changed, catching the attention of others. He purposely avoided eye-contact with others and when someone said hello, he didn't reply.

He returned with a sack of groceries and again, he said nothing. From this point on, Roy stayed in his room, rarely leaving. He barely ate. No one knew Mr. Thompson well enough to ask him his status or what caused him to be so different. Therefore, no one knew that on the seventh day of his stay, Mr. Thompson had learned that his wife had died in a terrible swimming accident. He cursed himself for leaving her looking for a better life for them. Had he been home he could have saved her from drowning. The emotional rollercoaster afterwards crushed Roy's spirit. Suicide did not cross his mind at first after learning about his wife, but it certainly became a notion. *How can I live without you Mary? I'm so sorry I left you.*

Often people considering suicide change drastically hoping someone will take notice and reach a hand out to help. When no one does, they convince themselves no one cares about them and their life isn't worth living.

On the 10th of January, Roy made his way to the roof hell-bent on being with his beautiful and precious wife again. He took one circuit before picking out where he wanted to leap from. From there, Roy ran as fast as his nervous legs would take him and leaped from the roof giving into his guilt and despair. *Oh shit!* Roy didn't expect his adrenaline to carry him so far. He fell until colliding with the skylight of the adjoining building's roof top dying upon impact. What had meant to be an expedition to find hope for he and his wife turned out to be the end of Roy Thompson.

The loud crash made from the fall caught people's attention, who then called for help. While on scene, the police quickly surmised that Mr. Thompson had jumped from the Cecil to commit suicide. Once inside his room, they did not find anything suspicious…or a suicide note. Mr. Thompson's effects were packed nicely, his dress shoes clean and at the foot of the bed, and the room overall clean. The open window allowed fresh air to circulate. His suits hung in the small closet and it almost looked like Mr. Thompson had cleaned things before leaping to his death.

This freakish event sparked heavy discussion about supernatural powers or "other things" working within the Cecil leading to the loss of life. Some even suggested a demented spirit pushed Roy from the Cecil while he merely took in the amazing views from the roof. Others suggested a strong gust of wind pushed him. The unruly supernatural entity that had disposed of Ms. Grace Margo had not been in play in this incident. Of course, no one could know this.

Local law enforcement worked to positively identify and learn more about Mr. Thompson hoping to see if they could figure out why he would commit suicide. They learned Mr. Thompson, aged 35, worked as a fireman in the United States Marine Corps until honorably discharging one month prior. Calls to the Marines were not returned. No narcotics or alcohol were found in his room. Next of kin would be located two days later after news of his passing spread and a family member reached out to the police. The relative explained that Roy's wife had recently died during a freak accident. After examining the scene and speaking to the victim's family, the incident would be ruled a suicide -adding another body to the uncomfortable list of suicides related to the property. Mr. Thompson deserved much more than what he got, especially as a military member and hard-working man who always tried to do the right thing. Fate, however, doesn't entertain or care about such trivial things.

Several suicides involved members of the United States Military. It's unclear why these folks gravitated to the Cecil. One thing anyone who studies suicide can attest to is that certain "hot spots" or "bucket list" locations to commit suicide develop over time (Golden Gate Bridge, the Doran Bridge, California's North Coast, etc.). Perhaps since other military personnel chose that location, they chose it too? Perhaps whatever fed on the souls of the dead at the hotel had roots in the military? Whatever the reason, suicide destroys everyone involved, and no one forgets when it happens.

Between 1938 and 1939, the area around the hotel, after taking a massive hit from the Great Depression, significantly changed. No longer opulent, no longer clean and devoid of trash. Homeless shelters and camps sprung up and the whole attitude of the area became grumpy. Strangers didn't acknowledge one another and crime, often violent assaults, robberies, and rapes, occurred weekly. The once gorgeous Cecil Hotel found itself choked by people it would have scoffed at and refused entry to just a decade prior. Rates had to be lowered, the quality of clientele declined, and the overall outlook became bleak. A decrease in drama, crime, and unexplainable events could have returned the hotel to greatness. However, fate roared in bringing along death and violence at an alarming rate.

May 5, 1939. Erwin C. Neblett, a Navy Officer, checked in. He'd recently been forced out of the profession he loved after an intimate relationship with a Navy Officer's daughter went wrong. She claimed he'd hit her, but truly he never laid a hand on her. Nevertheless, as low man on the totem pole, and the salacious story of him being an abuser running through the barracks and base, the Navy "had no choice" but to boot him. The moment he realized his beloved career ended became the worst moment in his life. He had no idea what he would do next to make money, rebuild his life, and try to keep his mind off what happened after he'd done nothing wrong.

Mr. Neblett's family and friends sided with his ex-lover. Coming from a long line of military members in the Neblett family, Erwin felt that he'd let everyone down, including himself. He did not do the things she said about him, but the guilt placed on him by others based on her lies made him want to end his life. He'd heard of people killing themselves at the Cecil Hotel and headed that way. Suicide seemed a distant option, but nonetheless it had become an option he never dreamed possible.

Erwin arrived at the Cecil and found the interior impressive. He had to negotiate a few homeless encampments and local prostitutes offering him a great time to get inside, but once there, the hotel did not disappoint. His eyes detected the cleanliness and attention to detail, a military trait he truly appreciated. He didn't quite see why others chose the hotel as a place to end their lives though, but on the bus ride up he'd already decided he'd end his there. *No one believes me. I have nothing left. What's the point of starting over?*

The following morning, a maid worked her way toward Erwin's room clearing people out who'd stayed past checkout. As she made it to Mr. Neblett's room, she detected a strong odor like that of feces. She let herself into his room and discovered Erwin unconscious near the toilet, his underwear down, and some sort of brownish-green substance near the lower portion of his body. Dead or dying bodies discovered by staff wasn't rare, so the maid did not panic. She backed out and alerted recently hired hotel manager, Robert White, who lost his mind after hearing the news.

"Send someone! Send Someone!" White screamed into the handset after calling for help. The dispatcher, Dora, a seasoned vet and highly touted trainer for the Los Angeles Police Department Central Division Dispatch program, answered.

"Sir, you must calm down. Where are you and what is your emergency?"

"Please send someone…I think he's dead," White replied almost in tears.

"What's your location?" Dora worked calmly trying to fish information from the upset man.

"Cecil! The Cecil," and with that, Mr. White hung up.

Dora dispatched two units to a possible man down at the Cecil Hotel and continued to field calls pending an update from the officers or a call back from the hotel. With an interest in the hotel's history, Dora couldn't deny her curiosity had been piqued regarding what just happened there. *I wonder what it is this time?*

Arriving units worked their way from the lobby to Mr. Neblett's room. They carefully made entry. The rookie officer asked the ambulance to step up their response. He thought maybe the downed man could be saved, but his training officer knew otherwise.

"One Charles Three, slow the medics, victim is clearly deceased," the officer relayed to dispatch while glaring at his trainee.

"10-4" answered Dora. *All that screaming over a dead body?* The life of a dispatcher, the unsung heroes of law enforcement, certainly pushes them to be callous at times. Her thoughts turned to her son's weekend baseball tournament and dinner with her three sisters Sunday night.

Officers cleared the room then secured it. The smell emanating from the victim caused them to cover their noses and mouths. After a more careful examination, the senior officer noticed the victim to be stiff like a board indicating rigor mortis had set in. In addition, the victim's bowels had relieved themselves, another sign of certain death. A froth of tiny bubbles could be seen in the corner of the victim's mouth. Next to the nightstand on the dirty floor were four small off-white capsules. The pills were collected by the coroner and later listed as, "Suspected Cyanide."

Mr. Neblett did not pen a suicide note. Since no one believed his side of the story, he didn't see the need to explain it all over again. The room appeared in order, there were no signs of a struggle or foul play. What little evidence police found pointed toward suicide. After being placed in a black body bag and lifted onto a gurney, his tragedy ended. His family would later learn of his passing and feel a tremendous amount of guilt because they had a part in his death. As a sadistic twist, his ex-lover tried using the same story she had made up about Erwin on two other men on base leading to the truth coming out that she lied about Erwin…and the others.

Erwin's passing served as a reminder of how people persist on this planet for a certain amount of time, walking among us seemingly normal and happy, then suddenly disappear having no impact on whether the world continues to spin or not. The finality of it all being a constant reminder to check on your friends and family to make sure they know you have their back. Humans and animals want to feel loved, without that, they see no purpose or reason to hold on.

Despite Mr. Neblett's passing receiving little attention, it nonetheless memorialized another suicide at the Cecil Hotel. Only time could heal such wounds, but eight months later the unsettling aura encapsulating the property claimed another victim.

––––––––––

January 10, 1940. Ms. Dorothy Sceiger spent some time admiring the artwork and décor before approaching the front desk and inquiring about a room. Staff later interviewed by police noted Ms. Sceiger to be "courteous and kind" and that she "had many questions" regarding the hotel's checkered history.

"When did they complete construction," she asked Susan Wellworth, a seasoned front desk employee.

Before she could answer Dorothy continued, "What was here before the hotel?"

Susan saw the line forming behind the woman and despite wanting to tell her just stop with the questions, she politely replied, "Well, the Cecil opened in 1927," she paused and continued, "And I'm not quite sure anything else stood here before the hotel."

Dorothy's eyes lit up, "Oh, thank you," she turned and gazed at the grand entry way, "Well, it sure is beautiful."

"Thank you, madame. How long will you be staying?"

"Oh, it won't take long. I'll pay for two days," Dorothy answered as she fished through her purse for money.

Susan considered asking the woman *what* wouldn't take long, but she'd lost interest in the encounter and needed to serve the people in line. The quicker she handled the transaction the better.

She handed Dorothy a key, "Take the stairs and your room will be on the left."

Dorothy grabbed the key, lifted her small bag of belongings, and took her time finding her room. She let herself in, dropped her bag, and headed straight for bed.

As she lay there, she contemplated life, considered what she should do next, and fell asleep within minutes. She'd been up for almost thirty-six hours and her body finally shut down.

The following morning, she awoke unable to recall ever sleeping so soundly. A strange fact since life had been so bad the last month. Anything that could go wrong, had. She'd been laid off, her husband cheated on her, a bus ran over her cat, and her brother, her only sibling and remaining family member, died unexpectedly. Of all these tragic things, losing her teaching job crushed her the most. The women in her family, as far back as anyone could remember, had always been teachers. The profession truly coursed through their blood. Being a teacher, seeing the smiles of the kids she taught, gave her entire life purpose.

Dorothy rolled out of bed more determined than she'd ever been. She treated herself to a warm bath, slipped into her favorite dress, and put on makeup. She wanted to look pretty one last time. After having a conversation with herself in the mirror, Dorothy reached into and dug around her bag looking for the poison she'd wrapped in a napkin. After locating the pills, she held them in her hand for quite some time as she stared in the mirror now completely unsure of herself. Her hand trembled as she tried to cup it to drink water from the faucet. *You can do this*, she muttered while painstakingly swallowing the pills. Tears began falling from both eyes after she took the pills.

Within seconds, she felt free as well as sudden fear. Reminiscent of Al Pacino demanding everyone's full attention in Scarface while wielding a machine gun at the top of his mansion stairs, Dorothy stumbled her way to the area overlooking the lobby, screamed at the top of her lungs something unintelligible, then stumbled down a few stairs before resting in a "vastly contorted" position on the floor. Those on scene immediately assumed the fall had killed her. She'd taken the pills to end things, but the pills and fall weren't enough to kill her. Not yet anyway.

Ms. Wellworth recognized the woman completely silent on the floor as the same woman she'd helped the day previously. She immediately reached for the phone and called for help.

Police were dispatched to the location on the report of a possible drug overdose. They arrived quickly and found Dorothy in a heap at the base of the grand stairway. She showed no signs of life, but they requested medical assistance anyway.

Shortly after, a two-man medical team arrived and began trying to save Dorothy. They detected a faint pulse and light intermittent breathing. The ambulance took her to Georgia Street Receiving Hospital -some on scene thought the transport odd because the woman seemed dead. LA Times reported her situation as "near death," while the police report mentioned, "appears to be suicide attempt." Since she made it to the hospital alive, the Cecil managed to avoid some of the blackeye from her incident. However, each time something like this happened, all the other random or dreadful events previously occurring at the hotel would generally come up in the news.

Dorothy resided in Riverside, California, at the time she tried to take her own life. Police did not spend time tracking down those who worked with her or her family to see why she tried to kill herself. Once a subject suspected of suicide is transported, police will briefly document the situation and move on to the next call. Typically, social workers or hospital staff call family or loved ones to advise them of the incident. In Dorothy's case, the hospital had no one else to call because she had no one left in her life.

An ER doctor worked feverishly to save Dorothy's life. Why she ended up on his table did not concern him, but how she did had him worried. Initially, the report read that she'd ingested poison, but no one knew the type. Without knowing what the woman had swallowed, the doctor didn't know exactly how to counteract the effects, so he focused on the damage she sustained during the fall…a punctured lung and three broken ribs being the most severe. He had no idea that the damage the cyanide had already done could not be fixed. No matter his or his staff's effort would revive the woman. The long teaching tradition of women in the family finally ended.

Cardiac arrest from the large dose of cyanide took Dorothy's life while she lay on the operating table. She likely felt nothing after the fall because the poison had pushed her body into a coma. The loss of her beloved teaching job proved too much. Without children, she saw no reason to live. Once again, the horrific and undeniable entity slithering within the Cecil Hotel claimed another victim.

Too much death and strange things happened at the hotel to easily explain away. Even though the majority of the Great

Depression had passed, things weren't quite right. Although that could be said for the entire United States at the time. As if on cue, the United States would experience strife on a much larger scale like what the Cecil experienced almost yearly.

A surprise Japanese attack at Pearl Harbor on December 7, 1941, suddenly thrust the United States into World War II. Franklin Delano Roosevelt famously stated the attack would be, "A date which will live in infamy." He received no congressional resistance to declare war on Japan. He and his advisors had the foresight to recognize Germany as a huge threat and the United States declared war on Germany shortly thereafter. Subsequent years were turbulent, but the economy came storming back when the United States and Allies won World War II in 1945. When the war ended, more than 400,000 Americans and 70-85 million people worldwide had died - making it the bloodiest and deadliest war in history.

For approximately four years, from the time Mrs. Sceiger passed away and near the end of World War II, nothing of note construed as negative occurred at the Cecil Hotel.

Perhaps the reports of servicemen and women dying abroad, or

the over two-thousand Americans who died in the Pearl Harbor

attack were enough to keep the Cecil monster at bay. Those

working there were hopeful the worse had finally passed, but

that wasn't the case.

———————

Peter considered all that he'd seen and learned so far and

briefly wondered why the violence appeared to stop? He

searched through his family's archives and noted that his great

grandfather, "Pops," roosted in the Cecil in 1945 while dodging

authorities. *Does Pops have anything to do with things calming

down?* Pops had no patience and could erupt violently in a

flash. He would have done everything he could to avoid

detection by law enforcement and smart enough to know

anything happening at the hotel would be bad for business.

Unfortunately, only he and his brother remained from the

family business, so he couldn't ask the others about this.

Curiosity grabbed ahold of him, and he considered getting into the room again. With the volume of information he saw in the short time while inside, he felt many more answers were left inside. His issue came back to Sam. *There's no way he knows I know, but he's here every day. How am I going to get more time in there?* As he worked out a plan, a bizarre incident in one of the photos caught his attention and brought him back to every unbelievable event that ever occurred at the Cecil to that point.

Chapter Five:

During the first week of September 1944, a couple strolled into the lobby and asked about staying in a room for a long period of time.

Ms. Wellworth pushed them as to just how long, "We're filling up quickly, how long are you planning on staying?"

The much younger woman, medium build and attractive, replied, "Oh we don't really know. Can we stay as long as we'd like?"

Ms. Wellworth nodded, "Certainly. Let's start with a week. Would you like a room with a bathroom?"

The male shook his head and answered, "No, we don't." He'd crunched the numbers and knew he needed to conserve money. They could not afford the extra expense for a private bathroom.

Nodding Ms. Wellworth added, "Fine. We have a room on the seventh floor that should be perfect."

After paying, the couple disappeared toward their room. Ms. Wellworth and the other girls began gossiping about the obvious age difference in the couple. During their small talk, no one mentioned noticing the woman to be pregnant.

Dorothy Jean Purcell, aged 19, patiently stood behind her boyfriend, Ben Levine, aged 38, as he opened the hotel room door. They let themselves in and became acquainted with the room and amenities. Ms. Purcell had previously been a "war worker" and Ben travelled selling shoes.

Mr. Levine made his way to the large brown chair and sat down. His profession had made him weary and his feet sore. He couldn't find a pair of shoes that withstood the amount of time he walked on his feet that were comfortable. Ms. Purcell made her way to the window, opened it, and gazed outside before sitting on the foot of the freshly made bed.

"So, when are we getting married honey?" Dorothy asked wearing a big smile.

Mr. Levine smiled back, "Just as soon as we can get established here and a place of our own." The couple made love and fell asleep in each other's arms. Everything seemed right in their world. Even her mom's constant nagging about Ben being so much older than her didn't matter.

Their daily routine involved Mr. Levine being gone most the day while Dorothy spent much of her time walking about the Cecil. She'd socialize with others from time to time, but for the most part, she kept to herself. She took a strong liking to the structures, architectural design, and layout of the main lobby. She felt immediately drawn to the mystique and rich history of the hotel. At some point she thought she heard voices speaking to her from the walls. She never told anyone this, until it had become too late to help her. When Mr. Levine returned each day, she'd brighten up and the voices would stop. Despite the difference in age, nothing remarkable stood out about the couple. They were not the only lovebirds at the Cecil at the time. Many people had "dates," girlfriends, or partners.

As a result, people mostly kept to themselves. Nothing about how the couple acted, specifically Ms. Purcell, seemed alarming. Only the sick voices gaining more control over her knew what would happen next.

Near the end of September, around midnight, Dorothy woke up and later told police she felt "tremendous pain" in her stomach. She retreated to the community bathroom down the hallway. She first attempted to use the toilet, but that didn't work, and she found herself on the floor crippled in pain. Within a few minutes, Dorothy gave birth to a healthy baby boy. She told a psychiatrist later that being pregnant surprised her, and she had no idea the pain in her stomach could have been a child. Fearing Ben would be upset by the commotion and the unexpected baby, Dorothy took special care to keep him quiet by covering his mouth with part of her now blood-covered dress.

Confused and scared, Dorothy left the bathroom, walked past a still sleeping Mr. Levine with baby boy in hand, and made it to the window. She quietly opened the window thinking she needed to get rid of the child. Something at that moment stopped her, but only temporarily. The voices said to throw the child, Dorothy, who'd been fighting the voices for weeks, resisted. But as had been the case so many other times, evil would prevail.

She made her way back to the bathroom where she gave birth, opened the window near the last stall, and without hesitation, threw her baby out, "because I thought it was dead." The newborn landed on the roof of an adjacent building and died upon impact. The noise from the baby striking the roof, and an eye-witness to the surreal incident, alerted people to call police. A murmur of the event coursed through the Cecil and panic struck -could a woman really have just thrown a baby from the building? Police responded with lights and sirens and made it to the hotel quickly.

Upon arrival, Officer Stewart Jones made his way to Dorothy and Ben's room. Ben, awake now, paced in the room shocked by what Dorothy had told him she'd done. He had no time to react or process the information before Officer Jones arrived. Ben later said his heart had broken upon hearing the story. He could not believe his girlfriend of two years could be capable of such violence. He always wanted a child and couldn't understand how anyone would do what she'd done.

Officer Jones swiftly placed Dorothy in handcuffs, a sight that also made Ben uncomfortable as his stomach turned and life had been flipped upside down in a matter of minutes. Officer Jones' heart raced, and he kept looking at the door hoping to see his partner arrive. He hadn't been on a call like this before…and wouldn't ever again. They didn't teach him what to do for something like this in the police academy.

Detectives were called to the hotel and adjacent property. They found the victim on the roof where the witnesses said they would. What detectives saw would never leave their memories. There should be no question as to how law enforcement members and first responders develop PTSD based on the things they see or must do daily while on the job. Based on Dorothy's spontaneous statements, and her terrifying actions, police later charged her with first-degree murder. Mr. Devine would never be the same. Dorothy would never be same. This incident would mar the hotel's reputation permanently.

The court case immediately grabbed the attention of the newspapers and radio broadcasts. No one familiar with the case could believe anyone capable of what Dorothy had done, but then they saw her at court. Her behavior and the things she randomly said made it obvious that she had something very wrong with her. The person most befuddled by the change would be Ben. Until the court case, he had no idea she's been communicating with deadly voices in the walls of the Cecil Hotel. Equally disturbing were the voices that controlled her. Similarly, those who saw her when she first arrived at the Cecil could not believe the woman being arraigned for first-degree murder could be the same woman. What happened to her while at the hotel? Although young, she seemed normal and happy. What could make someone throw their newborn child to its death? Alienists, known today as psychiatrists, were assigned to the murder investigation of baby John Doe. All three psychiatrists interviewed Dorothy. Each of them agreed Ms. Purcell exhibited signs of being "mentally confused" at the time she committed murder. This conclusion would change the complexion of the case moving forward.

A discrepancy of what Dorothy had really done came out in court. She told the coroner's jury that she threw the baby outside *their bedroom* window. Based on the investigation and trajectory of the victim, it appeared more likely that she threw him from the community bathroom window instead of what she originally stated. The fact she confused things became common during the trial, and based on her mental capacity, she probably believed she used the bedroom window at the time she committed the crime. She never showed remorse and appeared devoid of emotion, also odd behavior to Ben because Dorothy had been passionate and caring all the way up to the murder.

Los Angeles County Autopsy Surgeon Frank R. Webb testified that the baby had been born alive having air in his lungs. This came about because Dorothy's defense argued she couldn't be charged with murder since the baby had been stillborn. Jurors consistently discussed after the trial that Dorothy's testimony shocked them and was simply "beyond belief." The jurors also found it appalling that her defense team suggested that the baby had been stillborn, and she should be set free. Her behavior and the diagnosis of the psychiatrists made it clear that Dorothy had changed. That she had no remorse and no idea what she'd done, made the court case that much quicker. She'd killed her baby, but the question argued the most became whether Dorothy had the competency to stand trial.

On January 6, 1945, the court and jurors found Dorothy Purcell not guilty of murder, "by reason of insanity." She stayed in the mental ward of General Hospital as the trial unfolded and after it concluded. Dorothy would stay until a bed at a psychiatric facility opened. She spent the rest of her life inside concrete walls oblivious to the damage she'd caused or the pain her actions bore on Ben. She never understood why no one else heard the voices she did or believe that they were real. She also didn't understand why Ben left and never came back.

The calamity of Dorothy Jean Purcell now held the title for most disturbing at the hotel. It marked the first murder, but it wouldn't be the last. Prior to the murder of Baby John Doe, relatively little drama had occurred opening the door to some people speaking fondly of the Cecil once again. Some of the original ambiance began to return. Time seems to heal most things, but this grace period would be short-lived. The dark menacing entity controlling the hotel would not remain dormant.

———

November 4, 1947. A man named Robert Smith arrived looking for a single room for one night with no bathroom. He paid cash, dressed casually, and appeared friendly. He had average build, blond hair and blue eyes, and described as "pleasant." Other than that, nothing stuck out as unique about Mr. Smith. No one could know that he'd come to specifically take his own life on the seventh floor. He'd chosen the floor simply since the last digit of the year had a seven in it. He selected the Cecil because he wanted to leave Earth in a grand fashion, and the Cecil certainly fit that bill. Recall that nasty number seven...

Robert had cold feet for several hours. He tried to convince himself there must be more than death as an option. He thought of the people and things he'd miss after he passed. He recalled nights with lovers and romantic dates, fun times with his friends and family, many of the happy times of his life. But like clockwork, every memory faded to something negative. Since his parents and siblings considered him a misfit, he saw no reason to persist in life. If he didn't feel safe at home, where could he go? Society certainly had little understanding or compassion for someone in 1947 who chose to live gay. At that very moment, he never felt so alone.

At 7 p.m., Robert mentally said his goodbyes to family - none of whom understood his lifestyle choice. Being with men truly made him happy. And not just happy, but he felt alive when held by his partners. Only those like him understood him and felt his pain living in the United States during that time and being homosexual. Many strides in acceptance for this community would be made in the country, but it would be forty to fifty years later.

Robert walked two flights of stairs to the seventh floor. He paused having difficulty deciding what window to leap from. I can't imagine contemplating such a decision. A few moments later, having selected an already open window, Robert pushed his way through the opening and away from the hotel. He landed on the pavement below. The impact killed him. What remained intact of his body, and the massive amount of blood, delivered a particularly gruesome scene. Those who responded would never forget the sight.

Police were called and located the victim's wallet in his trouser pocket. Aged 35, on the younger side of life, many wondered what drove the man to jump? He had a comb and a little cash in his other pockets. When police checked his room, they located no signs of foul play and no suicide note. Other than his identification card, police had nothing to run with to attempt to piece together the puzzle of Mr. Smith and his probable suicide. Therefore, the brief police report had nothing left to offer, and no further investigation would be conducted. The official coroner's report listed the cause of death as suicide. And just like that, another person had come and gone. The building remained, but its reputation became further shattered.

Strangely enough, the passing of Mr. Smith began one of the longer dry spells of death at the Cecil. From 1947 to

1954, no significant event ensued within, from, or outside the hotel. However, the quality of clientele again dipped, and the type of people found living in tent cities outside the hotel property -as well inside the hotel- were no longer wealthy. In fact, most were poor and lived a life of crime. This portion of Los Angeles experienced no growth, money did not flow like it once did, and homeless people were piling up.

Hotel owners suddenly realized "Skid Row" surrounded the property. The rooms,
public bathrooms, private bathrooms, and building itself were beyond weathered and in need of repair. Time had been quite hard on the Cecil. Investors spent some money hoping a quick make-shift facelift would help, but no matter what they tried, the property had become the home of transients, drug dealers, vagrants, and nefarious individuals. The Cecil now required something terrible or sensational to occur to remain relevant. Negativity had become the norm and if things were too quiet, it

made people very nervous. Sure enough, death found a way to place the Cecil on the map again.

———————

Peter minimized the photo and opened the text function on his I-phone.

"Bro, there's some crazy shit going on at the C."

"What you mean?"

"Are you free?"

"Sure. I'll be there in 15."

"Cool. C U in a bit."

His much older brother, Thomas, had the most knowledge of the family and their roots at the Cecil. If anyone could shed some light on this topic, it would be Thomas. Peter suspected his father and grandfather of being involved with keeping things low-key at the hotel but wanted proof. He also would ask Thomas or use him to help him gain access to the room downstairs. He didn't think Sam to be a threat, but that would prove to be a big mistake.

While he waited for Thomas, he reopened his photos and spotted another one that caught his eye.

Chapter Six:

On October 17, 1954, Margaret Brown, heavy set with medium length brown hair and an unsteady gait, made her way to the front desk.

Ms. Wellworth eyed her wearily sensing the woman might be a problem, "Hello Ma'am, how are you this fine day?"

Ms. Brown took in a deep breath then answered, "Hello, dear. I'm afraid I'm not quite sure how I am."

Puzzled, Ms. Wellworth replied, "Oh, dear. Is there anything I can do to make things better?" She'd completely misread the woman and felt guilty for assuming things about her without even speaking to her first. *Geez, I hope she doesn't jump* she said to herself half-jokingly. Silly one could make a joke about death, but she'd worked at the Cecil way too long.

"Oh honey, everything will sort itself out. Can I please secure a room for one week?"

"No problem," Suzan scrolled through the available room cards and bypassed any on the seventh floor. *That floor is cursed.* "Ah, here we go," she retrieved a key and handed it to Ms. Brown.

"Thank you, honey." Ms. Brown took another long breath, appeared to mentally gather herself, then made her way to her room.

Investors spent money improving things and began advertising again bringing more people, but the kind of people showing up became a crap-shoot. Except for the staff, no one else paid attention to those coming or going. If the bills were paid, and the investors made some sort of minimal return, no one asked questions. Likewise, since criminals and low-life individuals with suspicious intentions had begun showing up, an unwritten rule of minding your own business remained strong and in full effect. Bad things happened to those caught snitching to the police or meddling in someone else's business. Nevertheless, occasionally a customer would show up that staff would take notice of and in the case of Ms. Brown, Susan decided she'd check on her each day during her stay. She made that decision because Ms. Brown did not fit the type of people staying at the hotel at that time and had no idea she chose the wrong hotel for her stay.

The first four days of her stay were normal. Ms. Brown woke up, freshened up, and retreated to the restaurant downstairs. When she had time, Ms. Wellworth would share a cup of tea with her and they'd discuss their shared interest in horses. On the surface, Margaret appeared happy. Deep down; however, she'd already checked out…at some point she'd end her life believing no other option made sense to her.

During their initial breakfast conversation, Margaret noticed Susan eyeing her diamond-covered butterfly brooch. While they sat and talked about the weather on the fifth day of her stay, Margaret broke the ice about the broach, "I see you enjoy my brooch."

Susan became red in the face and tried to cover her obvious affinity, "You caught me. It is so beautiful. I used to catch butterflies as a kid."

Stroking the brooch Margaret smiled, "My late husband gave it to me on our first

anniversary. We were married for thirty-one years," she paused as memories of Arnold flooded her mind.

"Wow, thirty-one years. That's amazing," Susan patted her on the shoulder, "I'm so very sorry for your loss, Margaret."

"Me too. He was the only thing in life that mattered."

Susan furled her brows, "Oh, there's plenty to be happy about. You have your health and friends I'm sure."

"Most of them have passed away, but you're right, I'm as healthy as an ox."

"Do you have any hobbies," Susan searched for ways to re-direct the somber conversation.

"No."

"Do you have a home?"

"No." Margaret engaged in the conversation, but also off in another time. She continued to stroke her brooch and finally decided. "Susan," she began unclasping the brooch, "I'd like you to have this."

"Oh no, Margaret, I will not accept that," Susan replied shaking her head.

"I'm not sure what life path I'm on, Susan, but giving you this, knowing you will cherish and appreciate it, puts a smile on my face…and I haven't smiled since Arnold died."

Tears formed in Susan's eyes, "I don't know, Margaret. This was expensive and a gift from Arnold."

"Honey, the greatest gift Arnold ever gave me was being my husband, by my side, every day for the last thirty-one years." She placed the brooch in Susan's palm and folded her fingers over the butterfly, "Arnold would have wanted you to have it too."

"I don't know, Margaret," she tried to hand the brooch back to Margaret.

"I insist, and I won't hear another word about it," she shook her head and refused to take the object back.

They finished their lukewarm tea and Margaret returned to her room while Susan returned to the front desk.

Susan found herself on cloud-nine and felt as though she had a new close friend. Margaret, although pleased about making Susan's day with her gift, had decided she couldn't go another day without being near Arnold.

In the early morning hours of October 22, 1954, Margaret made her way to the seventh floor, found an open window, and jumped. The seventh floor seduces the weak, then casts them to their dissolution. Margaret's body landed on top of the Cecil marquee, smashing the sign into tiny pieces. Many people had jumped from the seventh floor, but none of them managed to strike the marquee. The impact disfigured her body and killed Margaret upon impact. Being without her life partner proved too much to live with. The way she passed away took away from the significance of their beautiful and loving marriage.

The commotion of her suicide reverberated through the Cecil finally making it to Susan Wellworth. She did not know the person who jumped had been Margaret. She called for help and calmly explained, "I think we have another jumper."

When the coroner and police arrived, they worked with hotel maintenance staff to get up to the marquee area. They located Margaret and looked up trying to figure out which floor she jumped from.

The two detectives looked at each other and shrugged. One said to the other, "Coffee says she jumped from the seventh floor."

The other detective grinned, "No way. You're on."

They searched the victim's pockets and located no items. Nothing else on scene provided any details so they made their way to the front lobby.

"Hello officers, do we know who the victim is?" Susan asked.

"No, ma'am, but it's an older female, brown hair."

Susan's heart sank, "Oh my God."

Before she could suggest the victim might be Margaret, one of the maintenance workers jogged up to them, "Susan, I think it's Margaret."

"She stayed in room 512, fifth floor," she replied breaking down in tears…the butterfly brooch Margaret had given her gathered her tears.

The detectives checked the victim's room and located an identification card with the name Helen Gurnee printed on it. The photo on the card matched that of the victim, indicating her to be 55-years-old when she died. Detectives had no idea why she rented a room under the name Margaret Brown. Paperwork inside her room indicated Helen worked at a stationery firm in San Francisco, California. Again, detectives had no idea why the victim travelled south to take her own life. Nothing pointed the detectives as to motive for her to jump, but Susan knew.

"Arnold."

"Wait, who's Arnold?" One of the baffled detectives asked Susan.

"Her husband. He recently died. Margaret…I mean Helen…couldn't be without him. Why'd she use a fake name? That's why she did it." Susan took the rest of the day off, but proudly wore the butterfly brooch to honor and remember her friend from that day forward. Up until her friend's passing, none of the other suicides had mattered. Now she found herself upset and distracted. *Keep it together, Susan.* For some reason the suicides from the past hit her hard. *They were someone's loved ones and all we do is make fun of them. That isn't right.* From that point on, Susan did not take suicides lightly.

The official cause of death for Mrs. Gurnee is suicide. Although registering under a different name conjured suspicion, she clearly took her own life. Her passing struck a nerve with several staff members. Her death marked the first time a staff member actually knew someone who died. In some respects, the amount they loved each other begged of romance. Knowing this, however, didn't help those coping with the loss of her passing.

From 1954 to 1962, nothing noteworthy occurred at the hotel. Los Angeles inner city and Skid Row continued to expand and attract transients, criminals, and those with mental health issues. No social services existed for those folks, police were overwhelmed with calls, and downtown Los Angeles showed no signs of improving. Despair would certainly find its way back to the hotel.

———————

Thomas rounded the block twice before parking near the Cecil. He and his brother had an understanding not to put anything sensitive in writing, but they had code words. "Crazy" meant they needed to meet in person. Because of their auspicious pasts, and the fact local and federal agencies tried to keep tabs on them, meeting in person rarely occurred. *I wonder what my little brother needs?* They hadn't met up in months and after their last job, things had been quite tense between them.

Thomas retrieved his cell phone. "97"

"K. Door will b unlocked."

The two shook hands and embraced. Despite being pissed at each other, family is always family.

"What's going on?"

Peter pointed to his laptop, "Come look at these."

"What am I looking at," Thomas asked as Peter scrolled through the photos he'd taken of the wall in the secret room beneath them.

"It's photos from a place you, me, dad, grandad, and Pops had no idea existed."

Thomas looked puzzled, "Here? In the hotel? What are you talking about 'place' we don't know about?"

"We'll get to that. Blow the photos up and look at them."

Thomas spent some time combing through the photos. He saw the same headlines that Peter had keyed on. He saw the strings, Posy-it notes, and other stuff depicted in the pictures. His mind began connecting the dots and he had plenty of questions afterwards.

"All that stuff happened here?"

"Yes."

"Didn't Pops show up here around '45?"

Peter nodded, "Yup."

"What the hell happened here before he came," he looked back at the laptop, "And during all the breaks in violence?"

"I'm not entirely sure, but Pops would not have wanted any heat on the hotel. Maybe he stepped in during the breaks?"

Thomas mulled the statement, "There's so much going on though," he paused and looked at Peter directly, "And so much death." Thomas had killed men, been around death his whole life, but he didn't care for it. He agreed with his little brother. *Maybe Pops stepping in explained the gaps.* He had another thought, too.

"Maybe the gaps weren't when they were here, but the shit happened when they were locked up?"

Peter hadn't considered that angle. "Shit. I didn't even think of that."

They began comparing dates of the events in the photos and the times they knew their dad, grandfather, and Pops would have been in custody.

"Son-of-a-bitch! You're right. Every time they were locked up, the wheels fell off at the Cecil," Peter exclaimed.

"That makes sense because there's no way they would have allowed things to happen that would attract the police,"

Thomas stated. "So, what's with the secret room and why is someone tracking all this shit?"

"The room is downstairs behind the laundry room, but it's got a secret door to it," he chuckled and continued, "I have no idea who's tracking this shit or why, but we need to figure out if we're at risk."

Thomas nodded, "Agreed. Let's go check it out to see."

Peter shook his head, "We can't."

"Why not?"

"If this wraps us up somehow, we don't want to get caught in there. We don't know whose room it is or what it means. But I agree, we need to get back in there to see what we can see."

Peter filled his brother in about Sam. They developed a plan to get access to the room. Thomas worked on disabling the toilet while Peter phoned the front desk. He specifically requested Sam. Thomas would keep Sam occupied while Peter slipped away to examine the room further. Neither of them felt they were personally at risk, but the situation merited more investigation. While Thomas waited for Sam, he thumbed through photographs in Peter's laptop. A red line and Post-it that read "Follow the Money" caught his attention.

Chapter Seven:

Julia Frances Moore travelled via bus to Los Angeles from St. Louis, Missouri in the second week of February of 1962. Seeing California had been a bucket-list item for her. She'd convinced herself the move would be the fresh start she needed, free of the small-town rumors about her and her cheating husband. She left town right away broken-hearted refusing to give him a chance to explain or work his charm. *After three times you'd think I'd learn!* She'd always been sort of a loner and didn't care much for her family. *I don't need anyone anyway.*

On February 9th, she made it to downtown Los Angeles. The bus driver gave her several options of where to stay...he did not mention the Cecil. After exiting the bus, she found herself staring at the massive Cecil Hotel marquee and decided to stay there. She dragged her weathered knapsack, inch-by-inch, until arriving at the front desk. The bag contained everything she owned, which now amounted to very little material items.

"Good day, madame, how can I help you?" Susan Wellworth's trainee, Jennifer, nervously asked the customer.

"Good day. I'd like a room please, for three days."

"Certainly," Jennifer scrolled though available room tags and grabbed the first one available.

"I'd prefer a room with a view, is that possible?"

"Yes," Jennifer wiggled the room key she'd selected, "This room over looks the city and gives you quicker access to the roof if you'd like to look around."

"Perfect." Julia paid and requested a bellman to help with her bag. She met the man at the Bell Desk and he carted her bag to the room.

Once inside, she walked directly to the window. *This certainly is nice.* She cracked it slightly to let in cool air. She'd been experiencing hot flashes of late and the cold air felt nice.

Menopause is no fun at all. She fanned her face and took in the view.

For the next day and a half, Julia took time to walk the entire hotel, speak to staff, and eat at nearby restaurants. Despite trying to stay busy, her thoughts drifted to Steve, her cheating husband. She could not make sense of life. *Why would he cheat again? I've done everything I can to keep him happy.* She let him back two times previously. She lost weight, did things in the bedroom to make it different and exciting, and didn't hold his infidelities over his head. To be honest, she still loved him. Julia couldn't see herself with another man… she didn't want another man, she only wanted Steve. They had their problems, but he had been good for her and their three children. He never abused her, and when they were together, nothing else mattered.

Suddenly anger seeped in. She felt sharp pain in her heart and chest. She reflected on how badly he made her feel when he cheated. Bits and pieces of when she caught him popped in her head. The faces of the women flooded her thoughts. She found herself staring out the room window clenching her jaw and balling her fists -this from the most mild-tempered and sweet woman one could imagine. Soon her head became filled with terrible, unthinkable thoughts. *Maybe I'll kill him.* She considered killing the women he slept with. Eventually, she knew she couldn't kill him…but she could wound him deeply as he'd done to her. *The inheritance. He's nothing without my money. If I kill myself, it nullifies the inheritance. He will get nothing.* A wry smile crossed her face. As quickly as the anger had begun, it disappeared. Julia found herself at that very moment in peace. *If he can't be faithful, he can't have the money.*

She took one last look in the mirror, exited the room, and climbed four flights of stairs stopping on the seventh floor. It's unclear why she stopped there. After locating an open window, she pushed herself through it, and jumped out. She struck a light-well on the second floor of the exterior portion of the hotel and did not survive the fall. A lone witness said he thought he could see the woman smiling as she fell. Word of the suspected suicide made its way to the Central Division of the Los Angeles Police Department causing two units to be dispatched to investigate.

Police and the coroner were directed to the location where staff assumed the body would be. The coroner reported, "significant blood, corpse difficult to identify." The victim had nothing in her pockets. The coroner did not initially notice the hint of a smile on the victim.

"Looks like this one died happy. That's a first," Officer O'Sullivan said to the coroner taking photos and pointing at the victim's face.

The coroner stopped collecting body parts and focused on the victim's mouth, "You know what, I think you're right."

The commotion of Julia's body crashing through the light-well ending her life wasn't funny, but Julia's plan to have the last laugh held a stronger meaning now. The coroner needed most of the day to gather all the body parts and remains of Julia Frances.

A thorough search of her room revealed the following: fifty-nine cents, a Greyhound bus ticket from St. Louis, and a bank book (a check book today). The balance in the ledger read one-thousand eight hundred dollars. In 1962, $1,8000.00 went quite a distance during that time. Police later learned a savings account, which held eighty-four thousand dollars, belonged to the victim. The officers shared these details with the detective on scene, which made him think money might have been motive for the victim's suicide. Normally the lack of money causes someone to end their life. He'd never considered someone having too much money as a motive. Then he considered maybe somebody pushed the victim from behind hoping to steal her money. These thoughts swirled in the back of his head as he searched the victim's room further.

No signs of foul play existed. A suicide note wouldn't be located. Police positively identified Ms. Moore with an identification card, which indicated her to be fifty-years-old when she died. Somehow news made it to Steve, who phoned the hotel searching for answers about his wife. The receptionist waved over an officer, cupped the lower portion of the phone and said, "It's the next of kin for the victim."

The officer grabbed the phone, "Hello, this is officer Gillespie. Are you related to a Mrs. Julia Francis Moore?"

"Yes, that's my wife. What's going on here?"

"Well, sir, there's no easy way to say this, but Mrs. Moore has passed away."

A long pause followed while Steve processed the officer's statement. *Oh shit, the inheritance!* His tone changed, "How did she die?"

The officer thought it odd that the victim's husband appeared overly calm and only seemed interested in *how* his wife had died and not that she died. "Well, sir, she appears to have jumped from a hotel here in downtown Los Angeles." The officer prepared for what he just said to hit the man hard.

"Are you kidding me? She committed suicide! This can't be," Steve replied almost in a whisper then hung up. He stared at the phone in disbelief.

"Hello? Mr. Moore? Are you there?"

No one answered, and the officer passed the phone back to the lobby employee. He shook his head confused by Mr. Moore's behavior and questions, but he didn't bother with it further as he had another call to respond to.

Ms. Moore ended up at the Cecil running from her pain but found even greater torment. Her final wish, that Steve did not receive one penny of her inheritance, came true. Why she chose the seventh floor is unknown. Her passing marked the ninth suicide since the hotel opened -not the sort of reputation anyone ever assumed to be associated to the landmark hotel. Steve went missing about two weeks later. The rumor that swirled around town involved Steve owing the wrong people money and now that he had no way to pay, he slept with the fishes.

A green string replaced the red string connecting the photo marked "Follow the Money" to another photo marked "Double Murder." A younger woman and an older man were in the photo, and if his memory served him, he recalled his grandfather mentioning something about this incident -but he'd been told the incident involved a suicide and dumb luck. *Double murder? What's this all about?* He wondered if the maintenance worker had lost his mind or maybe a conspiracy theorist.

———

October 11, 1962. Mr. Dewey Otton and his wife Pauline arrived in a state of friction. Mr. Otton paid for a room and the couple barely spoke when checking in. Staff detected angst between the two, but they did not inquire further. After paying, Mr. Otton left the hotel and Pauline went to their room.

Mr. Otton returned around 9 a.m. the following morning. Almost immediately after he entered their room, a heated argument ensued.

"You don't love me anymore!" Pauline screamed in a slur. Her eyes were bloodshot and watery. Her breath reeked of alcohol.

"You're the one with the drinking problem, not me," Dewey answered in a roar.

She threw a bottle of whisky, but not before taking another long swig of it. "You drove me to drink! You're never there for me. I have no friends. What was I supposed to do?"

"I gave you a home, who else is making money for us?" he tried to defend himself against his irate and drunk wife.

"All you care about is money! Not me," she hiccupped and waved her fist, "Well guess what, we're broke. I spent everything!"

Mr. Otton pounded his fist on the end table and glared at Pauline. *I can't believe her. I need to leave.* He abruptly turned, let himself out, slammed the door behind him, and left. *She needs to sleep it off. I'll come back after supper. Hopefully she won't be drunk then.*

While on his walk to decompress, Dewey decided he needed to get her help. He loved her, he needed her, but alcohol destroyed their relationship.

Almost as soon as Dewey sat down for dinner, Pauline began writing a note.

Dewey,

I hate you. I hate everything about you.

You will never care about anything or anyone besides money.

Farewell,

P-

After finishing the note, Pauline pushed herself up from the bed, woozy and unstable, and shuffled over to the window. She looked back at the note on the pillow then let herself fall from the window. Tragically, her life would not be the only one she would take with her drastic decision.

Mr. George Gianinni, aged 65, walked along the sidewalk in front of the Cecil Hotel panhandling for his next meal at the precise moment Pauline jumped. He'd lived on the streets for years after being hit hard with financial woes related to his gambling addiction. He could not have known Pauline was plummeting toward him. She landed directly on top of George, killing both instantly. Remarkably, no one saw the unbelievable event unfold. When the police and coroner arrived and initially assessed the scene, they speculated the victims had jumped together -an uncommon ideation. What occurred had been even more remarkable.

After the coroner moved articles of clothing and searched the entanglement of corpses further, he positively identified the male from an identification card in his trouser pocket. Mr. Gianinni's hands were in his pockets and his shoes were still on at the time of his death. Based on the coroner's experience, it seemed unlikely that the victims jumped together because Mr. Gianinni's hands would not have remained in his pockets and his shoes would have flown off during the fall. Meanwhile, police within the couple's room had located a suicide note the female had written indicating a possible fight. Mr. Gianinni had been the result of terrible luck -which made some sense since it had been a gambling problem that landed him on the streets in the first place.

Dewey rounded the corner more assured of his marriage and full of positivity about getting Pauline help. He stopped behind caution tape wondering what had happened outside the hotel. Whispers in the small crowd of onlookers indicated someone had jumped from the hotel…some said two people jumped at the same time. It wasn't until he found himself being approached by an officer that he thought the situation had anything to do with him…or Pauline.

"Sir, I'm sorry to ask, but are you Mr. Otton?"

Dewey's heart pounded, "Why yes, I am. What's wrong?"

Sheepishly the officer replied, "I'm sorry sir, but we believe one of the victims," the officer looked over toward the ambulance and patrol car where the bodies were, "is your wife."

"What? What are you talking about?" Dewey tried to run toward the scene, but the officer and a detective who'd walked up to him embraced him. They had a difficult time holding him back.

"I'm sorry sir, you cannot run in there. We will escort you."

Dewey instantly recognized Pauline's peach-colored pastel dress. He fell to his knees and sobbed. The officer and detective knew by his reaction that one of the victims would be Pauline Otton. Dewey would beat himself up for years for failing his beloved wife. Over time, he found the courage to forgive himself and move on. But the last fight he had with

Pauline, and what happened afterward, gave him nightmares for the rest of his life.

The knock on the door pulled Thomas back from daydreaming. *How the hell did we not know about all these cases? And what does Sam have to do with it?*

He checked the peep hole and saw a man that looked like the man his brother described as Sam. He reached for his waistband for the Springfield HD semi-automatic pistol, felt it, then opened the door.

"Hello, are you Sam?"

"I am," he had a questioning look.

"I'm Peter's brother, he had to go to the store so I'm filling in for him."

"Oh, got it. So, what's the issue?"

"The toilet. I think I may have broken it."

"Oh. How so?"

"Peter asked me to look at it because it isn't flushing right, but I'm not a plumber. Now it doesn't flush at all."

He opened the door wider. Sam walked back to the bathroom to assess the toilet. As he began taking the toilet tank top off, Thomas returned to the pictures in the laptop. *I can see how these caught Peter's attention. I wonder what else is down there?*

Sam could see that the tank lost water because the flapper didn't prevent water from escaping the tank. Even rubber flappers deteriorate over time. He shut the water off, grabbed a screwdriver, and retrieved the flap. He rinsed it off in the sink and thought it looked as though someone had intentionally cut it.

"Hey sir, did you cut the flapper when you were trying to fix the toilet?"

Thomas wore a grin, "What's a flapper?"

Sam rolled his eyes. *Maybe his brother had...or someone else.* "Come here, I'll show you."

"I'll be right there, just finishing this work email."

Sam took the opportunity to retrieve his cell phone and check his own emails. He didn't know how much time passed, but something told him the man in the kitchen should have come to the bathroom by now.

"Sir? Are you still there?"

"Yes, sorry. I'm coming now." Sam had no idea the man manipulated his time while Peter scoured the hiding spot for clues.

Thomas expertly stalled, asked questions, and pointed out issues in the room to keep Sam at bay. He also fed Peter updates via text.

"You got about 5-10 minutes before dude loses it."

"K."

"Anything good?"

"Maybe."

"K."

"B up in a bit."

Thomas let Sam out and returned to a photo of a headline that read, "Local Woman Stabbed and Murdered at the Cecil." Apparently, a woman who lived in the hotel and loved pigeons had been killed in her hotel room. The man who police caught and charged with the murder did not remain in custody. *Lucky bastard. How'd he beat a murder charge?*

Chapter Eight:

Suicide had become common at the Cecil, but the case of Pauline and George, while bizarre and tragic, rocked everyone. This was the eleventh time since 1931 that someone took their own life, but the circumstances around the event were unbelievable. People joked that people within or near the Cecil were not safe. Suicide turned the buzz sour. It isn't fair to say people were becoming numb to the loss of life associated to the hotel, but death didn't seem foreign anymore. Not enough time would pass to allow people to heal before the next terrible event happened. This time, a long-time resident would be found raped, beaten, stabbed, and murdered.

In the summer of 1958, Goldie Osgood, later affectionately known as "Pigeon Goldie," made the Cecil her new home. Within a few weeks of moving in, Ms. Osgood discovered Pershing Square and a large group of pigeons she became fond of. She'd recently retired as a telephone operator and enjoyed spending time in the downtown area of Los

Angeles despite the abundance of homeless people living there. She took every opportunity she had to speak to people and tried to offer them support or food. Whenever she felt down, she would find peace hanging out with the birds. Where others saw them as a nuisance, she saw the pesky birds as stress relief. A certain bit of calmness came to her from the pigeons.

Polite, usually kind (but if you crossed her, you never heard the end of it), Goldie bothered no one. Goldie often wore a blue Los Angeles Dodger baseball cap and carried birdseed in a small brown paper bag. If anyone described meeting or speaking to a woman in the downtown area wearing a blue LA cap or feeding birds, they were always speaking about Goldie. As such, the cap and bag of seed became synonymous with Ms. Osgood. She sung with the birds and later became a staunch supporter of Pershing Square.

Goldie resided in the Cecil for six years. There's not one documented issue with her and anyone inside or outside the hotel. She always paid her bill and maintained her room nicely.

Having little money and on a fixed income made it more difficult for her to share with others, but she always found a way to brighten someone's day. She'd learned the art of communication as a telephone operator. She lived her life in this way and consequently had numerous friends.

On June 4, 1964, Goldie woke up early, filled her pockets and brown paper bag with bird seed and set out on the ten-minute walk to Pershing Square. She fed birds, visited with friends, had lunch, and returned around 7 p.m. She took the elevator to the seventh floor, and eagerly let herself into her room hoping to wash up quick and go to bed. Each one of the walks were becoming more laborious, but she would not consider ending her routine…deep down the walks were all she had left.

At approximately 7:15 p.m., a male employee delivering phone directories knocked on Goldie's door and noticed it opened slightly when he did. The door opening shocked him, because he knew she would shut and lock it when alone. This hadn't always been the case, but life inside the hotel had become tougher over the years. He pushed the door open and quickly noticed human legs on the floor. The torso and upper portion were blocked by a small wall leading toward the toilet. He missed the blood on the body and the fact the woman's panties were pulled down around her calves. Knowing Goldie lived in the room and being friends with her for years, the man compelled himself to venture further in. He rounded the corner and saw Goldie's death stare looking at him forcing his heart to stop. *Poor Goldie! What happened to you? Oh my God, maybe the killer is still here?* He turned and bolted through the door headed for the lobby. Within minutes, police arrived on the report of Goldie Osgood being murdered at the Cecil Hotel.

Detective Peter Towns, a senior homicide detective from the Central Division of the Los Angeles Police Department, got assigned the call. After arriving, he began systematically searching the room with his eyes. He noticed a weathered blue Los Angeles Dodger's baseball cap by the victim's thigh. Next to her head, a brown paper bag half-full of birdseed. The victim's shirt and pants appeared torn. The shirt was under the victim's mid-section, while the pants were on the bed above her head. The end table had been knocked over, a book thrown or knocked to the floor, and the victim's hands had fresh defensive wounds on the knuckles confirming a serious struggle between her and her attacker had occurred. Dresser drawers were open, the closet had clothes hanging in it with pockets pulled out, there were clothes on the closet floor, and the bathroom drawers were rifled through indicating robbery as a possible motive.

The victim, positively identified as Goldie Osgood, had been through a horrific ordeal before being killed. Det. Towns donned a pair of gloves and slowly entered the victim's room. The victim had a stab wound near her left breast and another near her left rib cage, although both would not have been fatal. Her hands, arms, and forearms had bruising indicating the victim fought the best she could. Her eyes and mouth had dried blood and her face heavy dark red odd-shaped circles where the suspect had hit her. A large bruise stretched from either side of her neck and a small hotel hand-towel located near her throat. Det. Towns thought perhaps the killer choked her to death with the hand towel. Police would later learn from the autopsy that the victim had been sexually assaulted. The news of Goldie's murder truly took everyone at the hotel by surprise. Who would attack a defenseless elderly woman who never bothered anyone? What were they hoping to find in her room? With the victim clearly elderly, the attack and murder seemed overkill for a simple robbery. Whatever drove the killer to kill her, Goldie deserved far better.

Detective Towns began collaborating with other detectives on scene while beat cops were sent to the downtown area to canvass the hotel and surrounding property for leads. Since Goldie had recently returned from Pershing Square before being discovered dead, and officers responded so quickly, it might be possible that the suspect could still be in the area. Based on the initial crime scene analysis, police assumed the suspect would have a large amount of blood on them.

Two beat officers walked Pershing Square speaking to people about the murder. Everyone they spoke to knew Goldie, but no one heard or saw anything related to her murder -a theme echoed at the hotel which bothered everyone, but no one more than Det. Towns. Valuable time slipped by. One of the officers saw a flash of white and looked up. The flash came from a white man running who stopped in his tracks when the officer looked over at him. The man then turned and walked quickly in the opposite direction.

"Hey, does his clothes appear to have blood on them?" One officer asked the other while tapping his partner on the shoulder.

Before the partner could respond, the unknown man began to run full-sprint and they pursued him. After a quick chase, they tackled and detained 29-year-old Jacques B.

Ehlinger. His clothes were in fact covered in blood. Immediately, the officers requested homicide Detective Towns via radio, who responded and took a minute to observe Ehlinger before engaging him in conversation. *Scared. Confused. Covered in blood. Is this really my guy? This is too easy.*

"Sir, why did you run from these officers?"

"I'm scared," Jacques replied with a shrug.

"Scared of what?"

"That I'd get caught. I shouldn't have done it. I just snapped." Mr. Ehlinger looked around as though he eyed an escape route. He never made eye contact with anyone he spoke with, however.

Detective Towns raised an eyebrow, "Where did the blood come from, Jacques?"

"Her."

"Where did you come from before," he motioned to the other officers, "these officers detained you?"

Jacques thought for a moment and answered, "The hotel."

No one could believe what they'd just heard. Based on his statements, it appeared obvious that Jacques Ehlinger would at the very least be involved with Goldie's murder. Det. Towns personally transported him to the police department, anxious to tape record his interview with Mr. Ehlinger. An hour after the interview, Jacques Ehlinger would be arrested and charged with first-degree murder of Ms. Goldie Osgood.

Any detective worth his or her salt knows the pitfalls of an investigation, especially during a murder case. A detective wades ever so slightly into the case ensuring every angle, every alibi, every piece of evidence adds up. Innocent until proven guilty still means something to the law enforcement profession. Almost immediately after Mr. Ehlinger had been arrested, Det. Towns' normally spot-on radar began to alert him to something not being right. In the eleven years he worked homicide, no other case went so easily. Although Mr. Ehlinger hadn't directly confessed, he seemed good for the murder: near the location at the time of death, covered in blood, and he said he attacked and likely killed a woman near where police apprehended him. After listening to the interview a few more times to write the crime report, he felt as though his questions might have been leading and Mr. Ehlinger only answered how he thought Det. Towns wanted him to answer. Det. Towns wasn't sure if the man played a game or had the intelligence (or lack thereof) to pull off the crime. *If he's so smart, why would he admit to it?* Det. Towns collected Jacques' clothing and sent it to the crime lab to be compared to the blood of the victim, but using DNA wouldn't be a standard concept in law enforcement until the early 1980's. Nevertheless, until the results came back, Det. Towns set out to gather evidence to prove Mr. Ehlinger killed Goldie.

Det. Towns chased down every statement provided by Mr. Ehlinger to create a timeline, so he could sort in his head whether Ehlinger truly committed the crime. Years ago, he had a case in which the suspect, with very low mental capacity, agreed with whatever he asked him. It turned out the suspect had nothing to do with the crime…the concept then known as truth bias, made the suspect agree to everything because disagreeing would cause conflict. The suspect did poorly with conflict and avoided it at all cost, so he falsely admitted to a murder he did not commit.

On the seventh day into his secondary investigation, Det. Towns felt it obvious that Jacques Ehlinger in fact did not kill Goldie Osgood. Ehlinger, a homeless man, had a physical altercation with Betty Brown, another transient. The homeless encampment they resided in with eleven other individuals had been affectionately called "the hotel" amongst those who lived there because the encampment stood one-hundred yards east of the Cecil Hotel. Det. Towns spoke to Ms. Brown and showed her a picture of Jacques. She confirmed he'd attacked her, but said she started the fight. They fought over the last bit of toothpaste shared by everyone in the encampment. Ms. Brown refused to press charges. She had a cut on her hand with three stitches from a fight with a bottle she'd lost. When she fought with Jacques, the stitches failed and ripped open, causing her hand to bleed profusely. That explained why Jacques had so much blood on him. Ms. Brown agreed to give a sample of her blood to be compared to the blood located on Jacques' clothing.

Det. Towns submitted the evidence and learned at the same time while with the lab tech that the blood on Jacques' clothing did not match Goldie's blood. Det. Towns made the sobering call to the District Attorney's Office to advise them that he believed Jacques did not kill Goldie. After his meeting with the lead District Attorney, they had no choice but to release Mr. Ehlinger and dismiss the first-degree murder charge against him. This major setback thrust the investigation back to day one, but the murder had occurred almost a week prior, making picking up the pieces and finding Goldie's real killer a monumental task. If a real lead or suspect isn't identified in the first forty-eight hours after a murder, the likelihood of solving the crime dips to less than twenty-five percent. A fact even more glaring in 1964 since very few of the tools used today to solve crimes had not even been invented yet (cell phones, the use of DNA, traffic cameras, etc.)

Despite re-examining the crime scene, re-interviewing hotel staff, hotel guests, and transients, and looking for other potential leads, Det. Towns found nothing to help his case.

Desperate, he returned to Pershing Square to speak to one of Goldie's closest friends, Jean Rosenstein.

"We were all her friends, all of us here in the square. I still can't believe what happened."

"Did you see the news about the man I arrested for her murder?"

"Yes," she paused and wore a skeptical look, "I thought he admitted to it."

"He sort of did, but he isn't right mentally. I looked into his story, and it didn't add up...so I had to let him go."

Jean didn't seem surprised, "Well, now what?"

"I don't know. You have any idea who would kill Goldie?"

"No." Her answer stung.

"You know someone suggested we get her flowers. No one has very much money around here, but suddenly, everyone started giving me what they could," she pointed to a large bouquet of red, yellow, and orange flowers in front of her, "So we got her these."

"I understand, Jean. If anything comes up or you hear something," he fished out his business card and gave it to her, "Can you please let me know?"

She put the card in her dress pocket, "Ok. We planted these because we just wanted her to know we remembered her. Please do the same, detective." Jean liked Det. Towns, but the fact Goldie's killer still roamed the streets upset her immensely.

With no suspect, no further leads, and no one stepping forward, the murder of Goldie Osgood went unsolved and eventually landed in the cold files. Det. Towns would never forget this case. How no one interviewed at the Cecil the day Goldie died did not see or hear anything during what obviously would have been a loud and violent encounter always struck him as suspicious. It's the one time that the unwritten code practiced in the hotel should have been overlooked. To this day, no one has stepped forward for a woman who had helped so many others, and that is a shame. She deserved better than what she received. That more than fifty years have passed since her death, it's likely the killer will never be captured, let alone identified.

Over a decade would pass where there were no further deaths or murder at the Cecil. Most familiar with the hotel assumed the string of violence had finally ended. Although things on the surface appeared better, internal strife crushed the hotel. Bosses couldn't afford to pay a decent salary, which attracted sub-par employees. Some of these employees were criminal. The upkeep failed due to lack-luster employees. The clientele staying there held little regard for property… or for others. Furniture had cracked backs, missing legs, or chips throughout. Certain sections of the lobby displayed peeling and outdated paint. The floors were dirty, the fresh smells found in the early days had disappeared, and overall the location could be summed up with one word…seedy. The once-lavish hotel had become a building filled with chaos, negativity, and consternation.

Peter let himself into his room. He found Thomas glued to his laptop. *Ha! He's hooked too.*

"So, what did you find?"

Peter produced a stack of papers and shook his cell phone, "I took a ton more pictures and this stack."

"What's with the papers?"

"Bro. So much has happened here that dad, grandad, and Pops never told us."

Thomas scratched his head, "I wonder why?"

"I think it's because we were meant to discover the room. It's like a rite of passage or something. Maybe they were keeping track of the stuff that happened when they were locked up."

Thomas looked baffled, "Why would they give a shit about that?"

"I don't know."

Thomas pressed, "Why was Sam there then? He's not family?"

"I don't know that either."

"Do you think dude will figure out that you were in there?"

Peter smirked, "I highly doubt it. The guy can't even remember his own name."

"What do you know then?" Thomas snapped growing impatient. The stories Peter had found in the room were outlandish, but if they didn't involve he or Peter, and weren't a threat, he didn't care.

"Shut up!" Peter tried to make sense of everything.

"I'm outta here. Text me if you need something or find some answers," Thomas gave Peter a bro-hug and left.

"Aaight."

Thomas posed great questions. Peter turned to the papers and synced his phone to the laptop to upload the photos he took to find answers.

—————————

Sam clocked out for lunch and made his way downstairs. He'd made progress connecting dots and wanted to run an internet search to confirm a lead.

He entered the room, turned on the light, and sat down. Sitting in the chair allowed him to relax. The humming also relaxed him. He checked the time and saw he had under an hour to work. *It would be nice to add this lead to Goldie's case.* His heart fluttered. *Would be even better if I could solve her murder.*

His group started when the first Cecil Hotel maintenance worker, Jim Stapleton, felt terrible that people were getting away with crimes and the police weren't doing their jobs in arresting the criminals. Jim's close friend had been smashed over the head and robbed. When the police came out, they asked a few questions and said there wasn't anything they could do for the victim. No one they spoke to wanted to tell the truth or give a statement, and the suspect had disappeared, so police didn't have many options anyway. At that very moment, Jim vowed that he would figure out who attacked his friend, gather the evidence the police needed, and cleverly alert them without jeopardizing his own identity. Since the group's inception, twenty-seven cases had been solved based on their handiwork and determination. Three of the cases were related to previous members being assaulted by criminals because they were suspected of talking or leading the police enabling them to solve crimes.

Sam clanked away on the computer keyboard searching for answers. He knew for a fact that the person who killed Goldie must have lived in the hotel. He, and the previous maintenance workers, had created a timeline down to the minutes before and after her death. All the evidence suggested someone had to know her daily routine intimately to pull off the crime without being detected. In addition, residents of the hotel had long held a rumor that she had a shoebox full of cash…only a resident of the hotel would have known of the rumored cash. The fact her room had been ransacked made sense as the killer would have been looking for the alleged bounty. Lastly, there would be no reason to kill Goldie *unless* the killer would have been recognized by her.

Sam reached for the stapler and something caught his attention. *Was this here before?* He lowered the light and grabbed his flashlight. He partially directed light near the stapler, that he never moved, and saw a very faint line of clear table indicating the stapler had in fact moved. His heart jumped. He looked at the dust again to make sure. *Well isn't this very interesting.* As far as he knew, only previous members of the group had ever been inside the room. His mind raced trying to discern if the room had been compromised and his eyes bolted open, *oh man, I hope it's not the fella in 409.* The sight of the moved stapler made him feel uneasy. *Now I need to figure out who's been in here.* Part of him believed maybe the stapler hadn't moved at all, but due to the group's sworn secrecy, he had to make sure.

Chapter Nine:

Peter scrolled through new photos and stumbled upon an image of a young-looking female with a Post-it labeled, "Suicide? Who is she?" He thought for a moment and again did not recall ever hearing a story like this while growing up. *What's your story young lady?*

December 16, 1975. A petite, curly brown-haired woman, slender in size, approached the front counter. She wore a long light blue skirt and a long sleeve floral print shirt that covered previous suicide attempts on her wrists. She registered as Alison Lowell, aged 23. Staff provided her room key #327, located on the twelfth floor. Ms. Lowell took the elevator and contemplated life. *Do I do it? Yes or No?* She decided no when she made it to her room. She switched into pajamas and quickly fell asleep. For the next few days, she tossed and turned contemplating the thought of suicide.

Ms. Lowell spent most of her time walking around the interior of the hotel. She'd bump into people and try to strike up a conversation, but no one engaged. Even within the Cecil, filled with all sorts of curious people floating around, Alison still got ignored. Hoping to find social interaction, she struck out to the streets. *What is wrong with me? Why won't anyone speak to me?*

The reception she received on the streets did not impress her. Being socially awkward is such a bitter pill to swallow. One is desperate to fit in, feel connected to the world, but no matter how hard one tries, being accepted by others escapes them. Alison could be described as mildly attractive, had good hygiene, and spoke kindly to others, but everyone literally looked right over or through her. If a transient briefly spoke to her, they belittled her or asked for a handout. She retreated to the hotel even more depressed than when she arrived. *God, what is wrong with me?*

On December 20, 1975, Ms. Lowell stood overlooking the view from her window feeling great depression and that her life did not matter. *Yes? No? Yes? Ok... It's time.*

After convincing herself she would not cheat death again, Ms. Lowell pushed herself out the window and fell to the second floor of the Cecil, which jutted out away from the main portion of the building. She died instantly, and her body parts scattered everywhere making her unrecognizable.

Police responded, but it would be Los Angeles Coroner Daniel Machian who processed the scene. The victim wore a blue and purple sweater, navy-blue pants, a navy-blue coat, black shoes, and a beige bra. Her remains were mostly unidentifiable and the cause of death would be ruled blunt force trauma from the fall and impact. A search of her room revealed no way to positively identify the victim. Coroner Machian guessed her age to be between 20-30 years old. A small black purse and yellow-metal Cecil Hotel room key were in the room. A Greyhound bus ticket from Bakersfield, CA from December 15, 1975 would be in the victim's purse on top of the dresser. Because the coroner could not positively identify her with an identification card or driver's license, and no one stepped forward to identify her, Alison Lowell is labeled as "1365UFCA-Unidentified Female." No one deserves to end life like this. Ms. Lowell escaped her pain, but at a significant cost to her parents, siblings, and friends. None of whom had any idea where she'd gone or that she passed away. In the 70's, as is the case today, an enormous population of "missing" persons flooded police departments with very few ever being officially located.

Scrolling through each new image never got boring. One image became more outrageous than the next. Peter had some understanding of a few of the cases, but clearly either his family had kept many secrets from him, or they themselves knew nothing of the cases on the walls in the secret room. If the Cecil had been their base of operations for so long, it seemed quite odd that his family would not know about all the incidents that would have brought police to the hotel.

As he slid his finger to the left, one popped up that he instantly recognized as serial killer Richard Ramirez. *Woah, the 'Night Stalker'! What's his tie to this place?* He followed various colored strings to the faces of men, women, and children. Those images led to other images of three obviously dead people. One Post-it read, "Definitely Ramirez." Another one read, "Probably Ramirez." The last one simply read, "Ramirez."

Growing up in the Los Angeles area, specifically the Central District, Peter knew "The Night Stalker" very well. Everyone in California knew of or about him at some point at the time he killed repeatedly. He opened the packet of papers from the room and sifted through them. There were three massive stacks, bound by big rubber bands, all labeled, "Ramirez-Never charged." *Well what do we have here?* He poured bourbon and sipped while sifting through the archives and learned he literally knew nothing about Richard Ramirez.

Another decade slipped by before the most evil and menacing person to ever enter the Cecil arrived. He arrived the summer of 1985. A young Hispanic man with high cheekbones, a terrible disposition, and horror-filled eyes slithered into Skid Row looking to dodge authorities. The look, however, had everyone fooled. Plain and simple, the man had become nothing more than an opportunistic coward. Fresh from another violent encounter with El Paso Police Department, Richard Ramirez chose seedy downtown Los Angeles hotels to hide and commit minor crimes. At one point, he landed in the Cecil. Once there, he snapped and became a serial killer.

Ramirez had an addiction for cocaine, sexual fetishes, and violence. This coupled with zero respect or concern for life made him the ultimate predator. He could be charming, but his intent later led to grisly murders. He'd get so high that he forgot to eat making him super skinny. His long black hair and clothing equally disheveled. What he'd seen while growing up, the crossed wires in his demented head, and the sheer joy of taking a human's life drove him to consistently kill. He would have continued to kill had it not been for the tremendous work by law enforcement to identify and capture him.

The hotel made the perfect fit for Ramirez. He paid fourteen dollars a night for a filthy room on the top floor. Local law enforcement rarely acknowledged the brick structure, which led to its attractiveness to the scum of Los Angeles. Just down the street, Ramirez identified a marijuana and cocaine dealer. Prostitutes, who he used regularly, strolled up and down 8th street, also right around the corner. He felt the dark energy of the hotel and took notice that staff rarely paid him any attention. He did not speak to many people and usually avoided eye-contact. No one had any idea what he had been doing. *They will know of me soon enough. Everyone will know. I am Satan.*

Ramirez wore button-down cheap shirts and khaki pants. He'd come back more tan and wearing a devilish grin when he returned from a day walking around downtown Los Angeles. He'd spend the day trying to take advantage of people, stealing small items, and committing petty crimes. Within the Cecil, he'd finally found a location where he could exist the way he wanted to without judgment.

From time to time, as his string of violence carried on, he caught himself lamenting on the brutal beatings he received from his father. No matter how much he begged his father to stop, he would not. Julian Ramirez, an ex-Juarez, Mexico police officer, lived filled with anger and violence. To get away from the beatings sometimes, Richard would sleep at the local cemetery overnight. Some argue his later fascination with Satanism began during his cold and lonely nights staring at headstones. Those who interviewed Ramirez later suggested it highly likely that his father molested him as well as beat him. Whatever the case, Ramirez turned to another male in his life to be his father figure.

Richard's older cousin, Miguel ("Mike") Ramirez, became his new role model. Mike, a decorated Army Green Beret who served in the Vietnam War, told many stories of exploiting women and showed Richard Polaroid photos of Vietnamese women he'd raped. In one photo, Mike posed with a severed head of a woman he told Richard he'd killed. At the age of eleven, Richard began smoking marijuana and looked forward to hanging out with Mike listening to disgusting stories of what happened in Vietnam. What happens in war has no boundaries, no filters, and for an impressionable young teenager like Ramirez, had no business being told to him. Mike taught Richard how to move undetected and how to kill. When Mike shot and killed his wife point-blank range with a revolver in 1973, Richard had been present. Mike would be found not-guilty by the reason of insanity and four years later found himself out of custody and influencing Richard once again.

With this sort of upbringing, there should be no doubt as to why Richard Ramirez became who he became. Children rarely can rise above beatings, drug abuse, witnessing death, sleeping in cemeteries to avoid abusive parents, and being raised in a culture of violence. If all they know is death and destruction, and their role models fuel the behavior, they grow up feeling like that way of life is right. Richard Ramirez took things to a whole new level and would end up being one of the worst serial killers in the United States…a fact he absolutely adored until his death.

One night while at the Cecil, Richard sat on his bed staring off into space. He rolled a marijuana joint, smoked it, and exhaled allowing the smoke to permeate throughout the room. He reached the radio and cranked rock-n-roll music as loud as it would play. The music and marijuana hit him simultaneously. He pulled out the small amount of cocaine he had left, snorted it, and began to consider what to do next. *Let's go play. Yes, they should know who I am.*

Well-versed in killing and being discreet, Richard committed several murders that evening. He broke into a home, shot and killed the husband, then raped the wife. After killing her, he molested their young male child but did not kill him. Up until this point he'd been a small-time criminal. No one knows truly what caused him to explode, but that night and the next few weeks had the entire state of California afraid.

He returned with his clothes covered in blood. He took them off, down to his underwear, and dumped them in the dumpster in the alley behind the hotel. He then used the back entrance and stairwell to make it to his room. He didn't shower or put clothes on. Instead he crawled in bed still way too excited from the kill. The fear in the victim's eyes and him being in control of every second of the last few moments of their lives successfully restored the dominance his dad's beatings had taken from him. He constantly dominated humans hoping to restore what his father had taken from him. He learned how to do so from his uncle, also a ruthless and sadistic killer.

The murders on this evening would not be his last. Each time he killed, he returned to his safe place, the Cecil Hotel. People wouldn't talk about him or to him. The police wouldn't come looking for him there. He truly felt safe. The evil that had dominated the hotel since opening its doors now found an equal with Richard Ramirez.

His reign of terror spanned three weeks. Fitting that the Cecil Hotel ended up being the hiding spot for the "Night Stalker," one of the worst serial killers ever to hunt within the United States. Each murder and rape fueled him to commit more. He killed women, men, and children. He used whatever weapon he could find or his bare hands. His victims often died bound, beaten, and sexually assaulted within their own homes. The victims were in their sanctuaries, did nothing wrong, and somehow ended up dead. Calling him a monster is an understatement. The satisfaction he gained while killing set him at ease and fulfilled his cryptic sexual desires.

Near the end of August of 1985, things in Richard's head became further askew. Paranoia convinced him that everyone watched him. The voices in his head told him everyone knew what he'd been up to and he shouldn't stay at the hotel. He made a run for it, but one week after he left the

Cecil, he would be captured. His perception of being followed and that police were looking for him turned out to be accurate. Police informants around the Cecil advised local law enforcement of seeing him at the hotel. Detectives positively connected Ramirez to several murders and attacks which had the entire state on edge. Police, trying to ferret out their suspect, released his photo which landed on the cover of every major newspaper across the United States.

On September 1, 1985, Ramirez exited a liquor store and thought he saw his face on a newspaper outside the store. He looked again and noticed his photo and the headline read he'd killed several people. Panic set in. Residents from the area recognized Ramirez from the newspapers, saw him running, and gave chase.

Ramirez tried to rip Angie De La Torre from her car hoping he could steal it and flee. Angie's husband, Manuel, saw Ramirez attacking his wife, armed himself with a piece of broken fence, and began smashing it on Ramirez. By this time, others saw Ramirez and joined the pursuit. He ran, but they gave chase. Eventually, the crowd caught up to him and some of them held him down while others began kicking and beating him. As this all unfolded, numerous people called police trying to alert them to Ramirez' location. All available units and an air unit were sent because law enforcement had become desperate to catch their multiple-murder suspect.

Ramirez managed to wiggle free from the crowd, jumped a wooden fence, and ran into a man wielding a barbecue grill cleaner. The remaining crowd caught up and continued to beat him. He chanted in Spanish, "It's me! It's me! It's me! I'm lucky the cops caught me."

Police made it to the location before the angry mob hurt Ramirez badly. He had scratches, bruises, and a few gashes on his head, but police ducked him into a patrol car and sped off to the Hollenbeck Police Station. Reports estimated nearly 500 people were outside the station screaming, "Kill him! Kill him!"

Detective Paul Tippin and his partner, Leroy Orozco, had the first crack at Ramirez. He did not waive his rights, so they could not speak to him directly about the murders they knew about. They did speak to him for quite some time, however. They both agreed that Richard Ramirez had graduated from a small-time petty thief to killer. They felt, based on his responses, how he carried himself, and how he looked, that inside stood a complete coward. They also had strong suspicions that Ramirez had been molested by his father. When they asked him that question, he looked defeated and slammed his head on the interview table. The Los Angeles County Sheriff's Department also interviewed Ramirez. They didn't get much out of him either. Oddly enough, they never (and still haven't) provided LAPD with a copy of the Ramirez interview from that day.

After questioning, Ramirez got booked and charged with numerous murders and attempted murder charges. Once Ramirez knew the police had to protect him, he returned to his egotistical nonchalant attitude and showed zero remorse for the crimes he committed. The public already wished him death, and his behavior after his arrest made those on the fence about the death penalty change their mind. It's fair to say most people absolutely hated him, which is precisely what he wanted.

After a long and drug out court case, during which Ramirez took every opportunity to act bizarrely, show no remorse, and taunt the families of the victims, the jury found him guilty of 13-counts of murder, 5-counts of attempted murder, 11-counts of sexual assault, and 14-counts of burglary. The jury ordered his sentence to be death. The ruling did not faze Richard, as death had been all he ever knew. After the decision, he laughed and replied, "Big deal. Death always went with the territory. See you in Disneyland." Ramirez lived on death row at San Quentin as a celebrity to some until dying of cancer on June 7, 2013.

_____

From 1985 to 2013, no known suicide attempts or deaths occurred at the Cecil Hotel. Nothing in the photos or papers Peter had suggested otherwise. A generation slipped by, the longest period ever recorded in the history of the hotel... much to the surprise of locals and those enchanted by the location. *Well no shit. Dad was here from the 70's to 2005, and I've been here since then. But how could so much drama, crime, violence, and death just stop? I've done nothing but hang out here.* He looked through the images and came across one that showed a girl in a dirt grave marked, "Garcia Murder." The image looked like it came from a professional and he wondered how Sam got his hands on it? It also dawned on him that Sam could not be the only person who knew of the secret room. *This stuff dates to the early 20's. Sam's easily in his late fifties. Who the hell else knows about this place?* He'd gone to the room looking for answers and came back with more questions.

Chapter Ten:

June 23, 1988. Gerald Lee Bishop, aged 24, strangled and drowned his girlfriend, Marina Garcia, aged 23. Marina had finally broken off their terrible five-year-long relationship. He found her bathing the day after the break up, swooped into the bathroom, then strangled and drowned her. *If I can't have you, no one can.* Knowing he'd just made the mistake of his life, he wrapped her in sheets and managed to get her in his car without anyone seeing him. *Now what?* He developed a plan to move her to the desert and bury her hoping no one would find her. He drove until stopping near Victorville, CA. After he finished burying the body, he drove back to Marina's Huntington Beach home and cleaned up the scene. An hour later, convinced he did not bury her deep enough, he talked his brother into helping dig her up and bury her in a much deeper hole.

For three days, Bishop hid at the Cecil Hotel. He figured no one would look for him there and he knew, based on other interactions with various local drug dealers, that the people staying there wouldn't ask him any questions or be nosy. He also knew the police stayed away from the hotel, which made it an appealing hiding spot. Gerald assumed the police were on to him right away, but they were not.

———————

Gerald had no idea Sam noticed him when he entered the hotel. Since then, Sam had been watching him through the cameras and on his rounds believing him to be criminal. Over the years, Sam had developed a keen eye, like an experienced officer, and he knew when he spotted trouble walking through the Cecil's doors.

The man Sam had been following phoned the front desk to complain about his window not opening. Sam got the message and responded quickly. *Finally, my way in.*

While inside Gerald's room, Sam worked super slow hoping to gather intelligence on his target. He remained cautious at first, but once his brother showed up, they talked non-stop. They seemed to be arguing and moved to the other side of the room. Sam then heard Gerald tell his brother, "What if I didn't bury the body deep enough?"

Sam continued working as they argued about what to do next. Over the years, hearing about death or stumbling upon criminals had become commonplace for him, so hearing the man say he killed a female didn't faze him one bit. He then detected that the room went silent and looked over his shoulder at the brothers who were staring at him.

"Hey man, how long does it take to fix a fucking window?" Gerald grew more impatient by the minute. Committing a murder and running from the police made him extremely edgy.

"First of all, there's no need to speak to me like that," Sam replied. He never let youngsters disrespect him. *Who the hell does this kid think he is?*

Gerald's blood boiled, his brother saw it, and stepped in. "Hey, my brother was just upset. He didn't mean nothing. Can you get the window fixed?"

Sam nodded, "Almost got it."

"Good," Gerald snapped condescendingly. The same rage he had when he killed his ex-girlfriend stormed back into his life.

The brothers argued further as Sam finished the window. He'd heard enough to make a call to his friend, a sergeant with the Los Angeles Sheriff's Department.

———————

On a tip from a concerned co-worker, completely unrelated to Sam the informant at the Cecil, officers began to search for Bishop hoping to locate Marina. During their search, they made their way into Marina's home and saw signs of a struggle. They were contacted by Marina's father who also said he "just knew" something bad had happened to his daughter. A theory of foul play developed around the same time detectives heard from an informant that Gerald might be staying at the Cecil Hotel. The informant gave them the floor and room number which led to them finding and detaining him. They took Gerald to the police station and questioned him. After they interviewed him, they charged him with first-degree murder of Marina Garcia. News spread quickly that a man wanted for murder had been hiding at the Cecil Hotel.

On May 13, 1989, Gerald Lee Bishop would be found guilty of Marina Garcia's murder. An ex-girlfriend of Bishop's testified that she overheard him say he wanted to kill Marina because she left him, and she shouldn't be with anyone else. Everyone knew Marina ended things with Gerald, but he could not process that fact or accept it. His attorney, David C. Biggs, claimed Gerald killed her in a fit of passion and should only be guilty of manslaughter.

"He will be punished like everyone else," Biggs said Friday. "But he is not like everyone else." Biggs also asserted that his client had learning disabilities and should receive lenience for his brutal crime.

At the press conference after the verdict Biggs added, "Bishop understands very little of what is going on. He only gets about a third of what he is hearing."

However, the jury, judge, and prosecutor Richard Toohey, disagreed.

At the same press conference Toohey explained, "He certainly knew what he was doing that day." He reminded people that Bishop had pretended he knew nothing of the murder he committed by showing up at Marina's father's house and asking him the whereabouts of his ex-girlfriend. In addition, Bishop stole one of Marina's paychecks and cashed it after he killed her. Eventually her remains were located, and the coroner confirmed the cause of death to be strangulation. Marina's father and family received closure but were never the same.

The evil that worked within the Cecil had called Gerald Bishop to a place making him feel safe. Police, based on several tips and top-notch police work, located and removed Bishop…forcing the evilness to call out to others to fulfill its insatiable appetite. Years would pass before someone answered the call, but the demons never rested.

Peter focused on the headline of another series of images related to a prison escape in 1995. He knew two people who had escaped, one of which remained in Mexico. He never knew exactly how the large group of inmates made it out, now answers were right before him.

On April 30, 1995, at approximately 3:15 a.m., fourteen inmates facing felony trials, including murder cases, managed to escape from the Pitchess Honor Rancho Facility, a maximum-security building in the canyons of Los Padres national forests and approximately 35 miles northwest of downtown Los Angeles.

Inmates pried off a metal plate in one dorm as other inmates in another nearby dorm caused a disturbance meant to distract guards. Once they removed the plate, a large hole provided a route for the inmates to escape. Prisoners climbed in and worked their way up to the roof. With the assistance of clothing and blankets, they covered sharp wire on the fences surrounding the perimeter of the property. Even though they got cut and injured climbing up and over, they jumped from the fence and frantically ran in different directions.

Four of the inmates were grabbed right away as sheriff's deputies spotted the large group scaling the razor-wire fences. Six more would be apprehended nearby, leaving four on the run from the massive one-hundred deputy and three air unit manhunt. Of the fourteen, one managed to elude capture and made it to Mexico.

Eric Reed, a 24-year-old man facing a murder charge, had been one of the men who escaped. He'd been in custody for a shooting near Gladys Avenue and 7th Street two years previously that left one man dead and three other people seriously injured. All evidence from the scene led police to believe the incident began when a drug deal went bad.

Reed cleared the fence and ran like hell. He stripped off his clothing down to his underwear and had some cuts and bruising from his run-in with the jail fence. He flagged down a driver near Magic Mountain and convinced the driver he'd just been robbed and beaten. The driver, oblivious to the prison break or the fact that a prison existed nearby, agreed to take him to downtown Los Angeles.

———————

Sam got a text from a longtime Cecil resident, "There's a man here, he's hiding in room 412. I think you should come."

"What makes u think he's hiding?"

"He ran in from the back and he was extremely winded…sweating profusely."

"Maybe he just finished a run?"

"I can hear him yelling. He's asking someone to bring him a change of clothes and said the police are looking for him."

"Ok. What's he look like?"

"BMA, about 5'10" med build with wavy short hair."

"Ok. Don't do anything crazy Cindy. Lock your door," Sam only trusted a handful of people in his life. Cindy, over the years, had become one. They'd known each other for twenty years. Although sweet, lonely, and sometimes a bit nosey, her information always led to an arrest.

He texted his law enforcement friend, "You know of any recent criminal activity in downtown?"

"Hold on buddy, there's been a prison break at Pitchess."

Sam calculated how far Pitchess stood from the Cecil. Although a long-shot, someone could end up in downtown Los Angeles while on the run from the prison. *Still, what are the odds the man Cindy texted me about is part of the prison break?*

"Gotcha. Call me when you can. Suspicious guy at the C." After pressing send, Sam took a trip to the Cecil to poke around and follow up on Cindy's tip. He also wanted to see if any more evidence of someone being in the room could be located. Before making it there, he swung by Best Buy to get a small nanny camera for the room.

Sergeant Tom Sears from the Special Investigations Bureau of the Los Angeles Sheriff's Office received a tip from an informant claiming escaped inmate Reed might be hiding at the Cecil Hotel.

"An informant thought he had seen (Reed) on the third, fourth or fifth floor, so we blocked off the stairways and elevators and started searching, room by room," Sears said. "There are 700 rooms in that hotel, so we knew we might have to look at a lot of rooms." The entire hotel went on full lockdown as a team of fifty officers blocked all exits and began searching the hotel room by room.

When they made it to room 412, they knocked anxious of the possibility of encountering murder suspect Eric Reed. People who escape prison are desperate and capable of anything and rarely go back to prison without a fight.

"We knocked," Sears said. "We had a key. We went in…He was standing in there with his back to us, his hands behind his head. He didn't say a thing. He seemed to know what we wanted."

They safely handcuffed the fugitive and focused on another man they had at gunpoint near the closet who had rented the room for Reed. Room 412 would be searched revealing a bayonet and narcotics. They took Reed back to jail and booked him on new on-view charges and placed a flag in his file as an escape risk. He'd later be found guilty of first-degree murder and three counts of attempted murder. He'd be sentenced to 25-years to life in prison.

The despicable murderous spirit with a chokehold on the Cecil invited Eric Reed, a killer, to seek sanctuary. Numerous other options were available to Reed as he ran for his life, but he chose to hide within the Cecil. People had not died or been murdered there in a while, but housing killers became the norm…an unflattering image for sure. Owners, staff, and those who chose to remain living there heard daily from outsiders that they were crazy. Some people couldn't leave because no other affordable options existed. For a criminal, the Cecil made the perfect hideout.

Chapter Eleven:

Peter became consumed by the room and what he'd found inside it. He needed to make sure that he and his brother were safe. His second goal became figuring out what the room really meant. Although his family had been rooted there for three decades, he wondered if they should leave. As far as he'd seen, nothing in the room had anything to do with him or his family. Likewise, none of the strings or photos had anything to do with them. Every crime they'd ever committed occurred outside the Cecil. What bothered him is that Sam, and whoever else, had been tracking criminal cases. *Maybe Sam is a retired cop? If that's the case, we need to disappear… like yesterday. I'm not about to get scooped up again.*

He texted his brother, "Bro NHL ended the lockout. Isn't that CRAZY!"

While he waited for Thomas to reply or show up, he skimmed through more of the photos. Most began to look similar until he saw one of a white guy wearing a devilish smile. He looked at a few more photos and followed strings attached to the man's photo and saw three dead women. On the first image a post it read, "Copycat?" On the other two photos were post its that read, "Jack." He didn't have any more than this and wondered who Jack might be and what he'd done to the women in the photos.

Johann Unterweger, born on August 16, 1951 to his mother, Theresia Unterweger, never knew his father. According to Theresia, she'd met an American soldier in Trieste, Italy, while working as a barmaid. They had sex and she became pregnant with Johann. Consequently, Johann, who later went by "Jack," never met his father. His mother would be arrested and found guilty of fraud while pregnant with Jack. Once released from custody, she made her way to Graz, Austria. When Jack turned two-years-old, his mother would be arrested again, this time for being a sex worker. Jack would be sent to live with his grandfather in Carinthia, Austria. A heavy-handed man, Jack's grandfather would take Jack along to steal things, including farm animals. Jack had no real social support and grew up in a culture of crime making his own transition to becoming a criminal quite easy.

Beginning in 1966, when Jack turned fifteen, he got arrested for various crimes including theft, sexual assault, and pimping. For the next eight years, he continued to live in and out of custody. Then, in 1974, now an 18-year-old, he strangled Margaret Schafer with her bra, committing his first of numerous murders to come. His signature became strangling victims with their bra using a certain knot that he always tied the same. The murder trial went quick, and in 1976, left Johann Unterweger sentenced to life in prison. While in prison, Jack's story became far more interesting.

Within the first year of incarceration, Jack began to write. He wrote a lot and often. He managed to get his autobiography, *Purgatory or The Trip to Prison- Report of a Guilty Man*, published and into wide circulation. He also penned poems, short stories, and plays. He wrote very well, causing artists, politicians, writers, and journalists to take strong notice... So much so that a quite strange thing occurred.

A campaign in the newspapers and political arena surfaced demanding the release of Jack because his writing clearly indicated he'd change for the good and had learned from his sins. In 1985, author and Nobel Peace Prize winner Elfriede Jelinek and an editor of *Manuskripte*, Alfred Kolleritsch, prepared a petition for then Austrian President, Rudolf Kirchslager, demanding the release of Jack. He refused to sign the petition; however, citing that Jack should serve the minimum of 15 years of the life in prison sentence handed down by the court. Although the political pressure remained high, Johann Unterweger would not be released until May 23, 1990 (precisely fifteen years of incarceration).

Jack hit the streets extremely motivated and on a high from all the support he gathered from people and social elitists that he now called colleagues. His previously mentioned autobiography would be taught in local schools and stories he wrote for children filled radio waves. Jack began hosting a television program discussing criminal rehabilitation and landed a job as a reporter for *Österreichischer Rundfunk*. As a broadcaster, Jack regularly reported on murders...ones no one knew he had committed. Jack had a secret no one would have ever guessed. Before the pieces of his latent life could be put together, Jack took a job sending him to Los Angeles -he went to investigate the differences in crime between Austria and the United States and how Americans viewed prostitutes ("sex workers" in Austria). The change in venue would throw Austrian police off his trail...but only briefly. Of all the locations Jack could have stayed while assigned to Los Angeles, he chose the Cecil Hotel. He paid close attention to fellow serial killer Richard Ramirez, which had made selecting the Cecil his number one priority. As a bonus, prostitutes flooded the area at that time -people to study then later kill.

While Jack resided at the Cecil, three local prostitutes were sexually assaulted, beaten with tree branches, and strangled with their own brassieres. Peggy Booth, Irene Rodriguez, and Shannon Exley had no idea they'd landed in the crosshairs of a serial killer. Jack knew Richard Ramirez had killed several times when he stayed at the Cecil, and he knew Ramirez particularly did not like prostitutes -a sentiment they both shared. Jack, in sort of a homage to Ramirez, took to 8th Street searching for kills hoping to recreate what he thought Ramirez would have done and *felt* during the murders he committed. Jack had become a copy-cat killer while employed as a well-known reporter.

Unlike Ramirez, who loathed law enforcement and suffered from a much lower intelligence level, Jack used his intelligence to toy with police. He went on two ride-a-longs with local detectives searching for clues for the girls he'd killed…they knew him as a reporter from Austria working on a piece about prostitutes and had no idea they were sharing a car with a serial killer. One could only imagine the thrill he must have experienced playing the police as he did.

About the time he hunted women in the United States, Austrian police began to consider Jack for eight murders in Austria and Czechoslovakia. That the women were sex workers provided a small connection to Jack. Eventually, though, local Austrian police developed enough evidence to secure an arrest warrant for Johann Unterweger for the murders of 24-year-old Blanka Bockova in Czechoslovakia, 39-year-old Brunhilde Masser, 31-year-old Heidi Hammerer, 35-year-old Elfriede Schrempf, 23-year-old Silvia Zagler, 25-year-old Sabine Moitzl, 25-year-old Karin Eroglu-Sladky, and 32-year-old Regina Prem. They were all sex workers and killed with their own brassieres. Excited to nab their suspect, police surrounded Jack's Austrian home and served the warrant, but they were left disappointed. At that moment, Jack lived in Los Angeles perpetrating as a journalist and moonlighting as a serial killer on foreign soil.

Jack had connections everywhere he went, and those who believed him innocent did not believe the allegations made against him by the Austrian police. As a result, someone tipped him off to the manhunt for him and he fled with his girlfriend, Bianca Mrak, before Los Angeles Police Department detectives could grab him. As usual, Jack stayed well ahead of the law.

Police chased them both through France, Switzerland, and the United States until the U. S. Marshals caught Jack in Miami, Florida, on February 27, 1992. While on the run, his cockiness ruffled many feathers. He called several Austrian connections and media outlets pleading his innocence and told them he couldn't turn himself in based on principle. The more he stayed on the run; however, the more supporters he lost.

On May 27, 1992, Jack was extradited from the United States back to Austria. He'd be charged with eleven murders, three of which were the prostitutes in Los Angeles that he killed while staying at the Cecil. The confusion surrounding the life of Johann Unterweger, and the fact some powerful people still considered him innocent, caused his court case to drag on. Dr. Reinhard Haller spoke to Jack several times and determined he had narcissistic personality disorder. The diagnosis explained much of Jack's life but did nothing to convince anyone of his innocence. The spark of his charisma had burned out and eventually everyone saw him for his true identity- that of a cold-hearted monster.

On June 29, 1994, a jury voted six to two (a majority vote and common practice in Austrian law at the time of the hearing), finding Jack guilty of nine of the eleven murders. The same day he received a sentence of life in prison without the possibility of parole. They swept Jack from the courtroom and directly to Graz-Karlau Prison, in the city of Gries. There were some people who were attracted to him and went as far as claiming police had framed him.

Due to the sensationalism of his case, prison officials housed Jack alone with no cellmate. In his cell, he weighed his options. He fished out the elastic portion of the waist band in his prison-issued pants and the shoelace from each shoe. He fashioned the very same knot he'd used to strangle so many women to death, wrapped the shoestring and elastic portion around his neck and began to turn around and around. The make-shift noose grew tighter and tighter until serial killer Johann "Jack" Unterweger killed himself. Jack had the last laugh, however, because he maintained that he would seek an appeal to the court's decision. Under Austrian law, his guilty verdict is not legal after his death, because the verdict did not ger reviewed or confirmed by a higher court. Even in death, at his own hands no less, Jack demonstrated his intelligence and ability to control his own fate while playing officials.

The text alert he'd assigned to Thomas pulled his attention from the computer.

"15 out."

"K," Peter responded. He grabbed a Corona, sliced a wedge of lime, stuffed it down the bottle neck, and returned to the investigation. A picture of a black man wearing a black sweatshirt that read, "New York, Fun Times, Good Times," made him spit out his beer.

Is that Kevin? He manipulated the screen trying to see the photo closer. Kevin went missing when Peter turned thirteen. He sold drugs then literally disappeared overnight. He'd come from New York and within weeks, based on his propensity for violence, became *the man*. He could fight too. He beat his prostitutes and shot several people in the area. He disappeared without a trace. For weeks people wondered what happened to him. People assumed he died. Peter admired the man and looked up to him briefly. Contents from the secret room shed light on where Kevin had gone…six feet underground.

September 1, 1992, 12:51 a.m. A passerby located an unknown black male adult in the alley behind the hotel. Where most places would be quiet, and few people awake, that wasn't the case at the Cecil. At any given time of the day, people were out and about. Los Angeles County Coroner Betsy Magdaleno responded to the scene to investigate the report of a suspected suicide.

Coroner Magdaleno noted the following: victim is a black male adult, approximately 20-32 years old, five feet eight or nine inches tall, weighing approximately 185 to 190-pounds. The victim had black hair, brown eyes, and most of his remains were unrecognizable. Without a doubt, the man had fallen from great height to cause that much damage to his body. He had a scar on the back of his right hand and wore a black sweat shirt, blue sweat pants, white undershorts, and a gray t-shirt with the logo, "New York, Fun times, Good times." Based on where he landed and his probable trajectory, Magdaleno estimated the man fell/jumped from the top floor or roof of the Cecil. Nothing on the man helped with identifying him, as a result, he became, "707UMCA-Unidentified Male." No room at the Cecil could be linked to the man fitting his description, and no one came forward after the death notice reached the newspapers. Magdaleno, based on the evidence at the scene, classified the cause of death as, "Accidental."

Dead bodies were normal for the area, so the unknown man's death went unnoticed. Joe Smith, big man on the block before Kevin showed up, knew this. He lured Kevin to the roof of the Cecil, so they could talk business. Leery from the start, Kevin did not like the situation. However, Joe talked about big money, and money ruled Kevin's world. He packed his Glock in his waistband, negotiated the stairs to the roof, and saw Joe pacing near the edge.

"Bruh. I'm not about to get close to the edge. Come over here," Kevin called out to Joe. *What's this fool up to?*

Joe waved him over, "You need to see this."

"Nah. Tell me from there." Kevin trusted no one, especially some punk he'd clowned day one on the block.

Joe grinned, "Bruh. You wanna see how we gonna stack racks, you need to see this right here," he pointed beyond the roof toward a fake spot doing whatever he could to lure Kevin closer to the edge. *Come closer. Bet I get your ass.*

"I'm good. What's the shit you talking?"

"We gonna work together, we gotta have trust," he backed farther away from the roof edge, "How bout now?"

Even though business had been decent, the police had arrested several of his girls forcing Kevin to search for other ways to make money. Even though he didn't care for Joe, the man knew the area and had connections.

He slowly walked closer to Joe, "Bruh stop the bullshit. We talkin' money or not."

"I'm talking 25k for each of us."

Kevin's left eyebrow went up, "25? Each?"

"Yeah bruh."

"Ok, what's the job?" Kevin didn't think any job would pay so much money.

Joe turned again looking out over downtown, "Mexicans down the block reached out. They want us to take out Lil' Pimp."

"Pimp? Why?" Internally Kevin chuckled. *I knew that fool would cross the wrong person.*

"They didn't say. They said half up front, the other half when he's gone."

Kevin wore a questioned look on his face, "So why you pointing over there?" he craned his head to the right, "Pimp be laying his head that way." He made sure not to take his eyes off Joe.

"Nah," Joe pointed at a building close by in the opposite direction, "He's over here now."

Kevin moved closer. Joe taking advantage of him didn't cross his mind, but he genuinely feared heights.

Joe didn't turn back around this time. He kept looking at a building trying to keep the ruse going, hoping Kevin would get close enough for him to pounce.

Kevin moved closer still, "They reached out to you. How I know I'm gonna get mines?"

"I'll have them pay you directly, man."

Kevin mulled the proposition and found himself interested at seeing what Joe pointed at. "When do we roll?"

"There he go right there. We can do it now." He inched his fingers closer to his right hip and grabbed the bottom of the taser and felt Kevin getting much closer to him. *Three, two, one!*

Without hesitation, Joe ripped out a taser, arched it, and swung it toward Kevin's mid-section missing good contact. Almost as quickly, Kevin pulled out his firearm and squeezed of a round hitting Joe in the left upper arm. Adrenaline kicked in as Joe desperately lunged with the taser, this time making direct contact. Kevin grimaced in pain, dropped his gun, and had just enough time to see a two-by-four piece of wood coming at his face.

Joe swung like he tried to hit a homerun knocking Kevin out. He cleared out Kevin's pockets and rolled him closer and closer to the edge of the roof. The pain in his arm became unbearable, but he had work to do. He got down on his butt, put his legs on the side of Kevin's unconscious body, and kicked him off. *Who's the punk now?* He struggled to get to his legs, texted a guy that could stitch his wound, and took off. No one ever missed Kevin.

Chapter Twelve:

January 8, 2013. After morning rounds, Sam grew anxious to get the newspaper article he'd found on a board in the secret room. He'd completely dismissed the chance encounter with the man he knew as Room 409. He'd suspected him to be criminal, but never found anything to pin on him. He returned to his mission: remain secret and figure out what caused violence at the Cecil Hotel. When they recruited him, he learned to collect data, talk to people, and gather evidence. At the core of his, and the group's belief, was that someone or *something* evil resided at the hotel. Over time, the group also helped police solve cases without giving up their identity. Sam became the seventh member of the group since it began in 1927. He'd been watching two of his co-workers to see who he'd recruit, but both seemed immature. He'd stay in his role for a few more years, so he had time to groom one of them.

He entered the room around midnight. He eagerly checked the camera to see if his suspicion of someone entering the room could be confirmed. At first, he let it play normal speed, but after a while, he got bored. He fast-forwarded through hours of footage and saw nothing. He turned his attention to the newspaper article he'd secured, pulled off two pieces of scotch tape, affixed them to the corners of the article, and placed it on the wall next to the appropriate spot. He inadvertently left the footage playing as he did this. *Shit!*

Sam returned to the computer, used the mouse to hit the rewind button, and his eyes registered pure shock. A man, wearing all dark clothing and a mask, fished through some of the cardboard boxes. *Who the hell is that?* His mind raced trying to figure out his next move. *This is bad. Real bad. Could it be Room 409? Now what do I do?* As far as he knew, no one beside group members had ever been in the room. No one ever told him what to do if someone discovered the room.

Thomas knocked on Peter's door, "It's me."

Peter let him. "Bro, you remember Kevin?"

"No, who's that?"

"Remember the guy from New York who took over the block then disappeared?"

Thomas thought for a second and his eyes suggested he remembered now, "That Kevin? Yeah, I remember him. Didn't he leave as quickly as he came?"

Peter chuckled, "He didn't leave."

"What?"

"You remember Lil Joe?" Peter, excited to share the news because he knew his brother would be shocked, wore a large smile.

"Yeah, why?"

"Joe killed Kevin."

Thomas stood there with his mouth open, "What? How do you know that" and before Peter could reply he asked, "And how did he pull that off? Didn't Kevin take his block?"

Peter shared what he'd learned from the photos and notes from the room. As he relayed the story it still seemed far-fetched, but Sam and whoever used the room had connected the dots.

Thomas still didn't believe the story, "Then why didn't Joe get scooped up for the murder?"

"They killed him before police were alerted to him killing Kevin."

"Alerted?"

"Yeah…so that's why I had you come back. This guy Sam and whoever else we don't know, use the room to solve crimes and track crime here at the hotel."

Thomas grunted, "So a bunch of snitches."

"Yeah, which means we could be at risk if we stay here."

"Why? We don't do shit here," Thomas didn't see the need to leave the place he, his brother, and the rest of the men in the family as long as he could remember lived in.

"I don't want to leave, but we can't afford any heat right now."

"Why," again Thomas couldn't believe his ears.

"I got a call. We have a job. It's here," Peter eyed his brother to see his reaction. He could sometimes go off and be a handful to reel back in.

"Here? What are you talking about?"

"It's a kidnap for ransom. We get twenty-percent. Some Asian dignitary's daughter is here, and her family is filthy rich." Despite the money, Peter desperately need an adrenaline rush and wanted to do the job.

Thomas thought for a minute, "I don't know man, doing a job here is sketchy. Plus, what if the guy from the room finds out? I'm telling you right now, I'm not going back to prison."

"Agreed. It's a huge contract though," he patted Thomas on the shoulder, "And it's not like we're rookies. We'll grab the girl, stash her here, get paid, and let her go."

"Here? Like in this room?"

"Yeah, where else we gonna stash her? Plus, they will never figure that a kidnapped woman would be in the hotel someone took her from." Peter had already given quite a bit of thought to the plan. He hoped he could talk his older brother into it.

"I don't know, bro. This is super risky. We've never done a job inside this place. And the more I think about that room downstairs, the more it creeps me out," Thomas replied. He truly did not want to get caught. *I can't go back. I'm getting too old for this shit. Plus, these gigs never pay like they tell us.*

"It's a quick job. We will give them 48-hours. After that, I say we split for good. Say goodbye to the Cecil." It sounded odd saying that out loud, but Sam's activities convinced him they were living in a trap and they needed to find a new location to run their business.

"This is the US. What makes you think they will pay? The police will tell them not to."

"True, but she's a *somebody* and her family won't care about American tactics. They will want her back and they will pay the ransom. I've done the research already."

"I don't know, brother. How are we supposed to get our cut?"

"Electronic transfer to our account," he poured two shots, sliced two pieces of lime, and grabbed some salt.

Thomas picked up his glass, "Salude!" They finished the shots and worked out the details of the job and an exit strategy from the Cecil Hotel.

Chapter Thirteen:

Sabrina Ma, the ransom target, entered the Cecil on January 28, 2013. The contact said she had one armed bodyguard with her. Based on how the man shadowing the target moved and his physical shape, Peter believed he could fight and assumed he'd trained in some sort of hand-to-hand combat. *This dude is going to be a problem. Good thing Thomas is a beast.*

The plan didn't take long to hash out. Take out the bodyguard, stash the girl in Peter's room (which had a safe-room built into it), alert the contact, then wait. The contact would handle everything else and advise when they received payment. If the girl's family didn't pay, they would let her go and disappear to take new roots... in Chicago.

Peter and Thomas surveilled Sabrina every hour for two days. A routine had been established. The most opportune time to grab her would be when she exited her room to get her morning jog in. The bodyguard would be waiting at the door ten minutes before she appeared. He would check both ends of the hallway and post up at the door. Thomas would grab him when he tried the emergency exit to the stairs, take him into the stairwell, then gag and tie him. At the same time, Peter would don the guard's suit, put it on, and post up at Sabrina's door. Their similarity in size gave him confidence that she would come out. *She's gotta come out, otherwise it may get dirty if we must go inside.* For them to get paid, Sabrina could not be hurt, and proof of life would be needed to fulfill the contract.

Like clockwork, the bodyguard left the room adjacent from the target, scanned the hallway, and walked toward the window.

Peter texted Thomas, "Out." He saw the bodyguard from the peep hole from across the hall.

"Copy." Thomas paced in the stairs like a caged lion. The bodyguard didn't need to get hurt, just removed for a bit so they could grab the target. However, if the guy tried to end Thomas' life, he would protect himself at all cost. Thomas felt his heartbeat in his chest and head. *Calm down. Calm down.* He double checked that he had his gun, duct tape and rope, and prayed.

The bodyguard made his way quietly past Peter and toward the emergency exit. "Headed ur way."

Thomas read the message, slipped the phone in his pocket, and lifted himself up slightly on his tippy-toes to see out the small window of the door. He saw the bodyguard's shadow indicating he was nearby -his cue to throw a flashlight down the stairs to draw the bodyguard in. *Clank, clank, clank.*

What was that? The man cautiously approached the door. Being too short to look in the window, the sound forced him to go into the stairwell. He opened the door and waited a second before breaking the threshold. Using his right foot to prop the door, he looked around the door and felt the kick before seeing it. He braced for the impact but clearly hadn't been ready for an attack.

Both men were excellent fighters and countered each other's strikes with blocks or other strikes. Thomas needed the fight to end immediately. The longer they fought, the more chance he had of being discovered and that would jeopardize the operation. The bodyguard throat-chopped Thomas. The force stunned him, but he managed to get behind the man and his massive arms around his neck and under his chin. *Game over.* He squeezed with the force of a machine vise choking the man out quickly. He then tied him and wrapped several rounds of duct tape around his mouth and a piece over his eyes. The man regained consciousness in time to know he'd been disabled, and his vision blocked. He moaned and thrashed about trying to alert someone to help him.

"Ready," Thomas texted Peter.

"If you don't shut up, I'll put a bullet in you," he spat his own blood on the guard -the effects of a punch that landed just above his right brow splitting the skin open. He pulled out his

Glock and put the barrel on the man's face. "I know you know what this is." The man stopped making noises.

Peter entered the stairwell, saw the bodyguard tied down, and panicked. "Shit! How am I supposed to get his suit? He's tied up?"

"Fuck, I don't know! You said tie him up!"

Peter tried to think on the fly, then heard a door open and shut quickly in the hallway. *Shit!*

He peeked around the door and saw a slender woman with long black hair wearing a red jogging suit running full speed the other direction. Without hesitation, he sprung after her and hissed, "She's getting away! Go down stairs!" The woman did not look back, and he caught up to her quickly.

She made it to the end of the hallway, ran directly toward an open window, and tried to jump out as Peter grabbed her around the waist. She screamed and kicked wildly. He covered her mouth and she bit him. "Ouch!" He covered her mouth again, grabbed a rag from his pocket, and replaced his hand with the rag while carrying her like a sack of groceries to his room.

Once inside, he placed the woman in a wooden chair, wrapped the rag in her mouth with duct tape, her arms and legs to the chair, and placed a black bag over her head. The whole thing took less than a minute. In the confusion, he never positively identified the woman as Sabrina Ma. The woman he'd grabbed came from one room east of the target. Her name was Elisa Lam. She'd made her mind up to end her life, and in a strange bit of luck (or misfortune), the man who had just kidnapped her had saved her life.

Peter retrieved his cell phone, "In pocket." He poured hydrogen peroxide on the wounds from the target and sent another text from the other cell phone on the counter, "In pocket."

Thomas took the bodyguard downstairs after the text from Peter. He located the secret room, opened it like Peter had shown him, and dragged the bodyguard inside. He left him there and retreated out of the hotel to a safe house. Both he and Peter were confident Sam locating the kidnapped dignitary's daughter's bodyguard in the room would blow the cover on the room and thoroughly confuse law enforcement. His task now involved addressing his wounds and waiting to hear from his brother. He grabbed packets of ice and a bottle of Jack Daniels. *He could have killed me. I'm getting too old for this shit.*

———————

A certain buzz flowed through the Cecil that Sam detected when he arrived. He felt it but had no idea what caused it. He let himself into the room hoping to estimate what it would take, both in storage space and time, to clear it out completely. Seeing someone in the room had been the final straw and proof the secret had been exposed. Sam knew his life could be in danger based on all the people his, and the others' tips, had led to people being arrested and serving time.

As the door shut behind him, he heard a faint moan deeper into the room. *What the hell is that?* He slowly walked toward the large wooden desk and the moan got louder. He considered running for it, but he wanted to know what, or who, made the moaning sound. *Maybe it's just some kids making out?* He turned the corner and yelped out loud. A man wearing a suit had been tied to the desk. His hands and feet were bound with gray tape, a piece of duct tape covered his mouth and eyes. Sam had no idea what to do next. *Run. I need to make a run for it.* He had so many questions and panic sunk in. Too much paperwork and files were in the room for him to grab and leave. In addition, when he yelped, it alerted the man of his presence, which caused the man to writhe on the floor and moan louder. *This needs to stop. I need to get him quiet.*

Sam got closer to the man and removed the tape from his eyes. He continued to moan then looked around trying to figure out his whereabouts while eyeing Sam suspiciously.

"Listen, I don't know who you are, but you need to stop!"

The bound man stopped moaning but searched the room for a way out. He could tell the man speaking to him had nothing to do with the situation he found himself in now.

"If I take the tape off your mouth, will you promise not to scream?" Sam couldn't entirely process everything going on in his head or in front of him, but if the man stayed quiet, Sam stood a good chance of no one else finding the room. He appreciated that the secrecy of the location had been compromised, but he needed time to pack up and move.

The man nodded.

Sam removed the tape, "Who are you?"

"There's no time, release me! I need to check on Sabrina!"

"Who's Sabrina?" Sam had a random man in his secret room who seemed confused and talking about someone he didn't know.

"Please! There's no time!" The man tried to get up but couldn't.

"Listen, I don't know you or a Sabrina, and until I'm assured of my own safety, I won't untie you."

"Please! I'm paid protection for Sabrina Ma. She's in danger."

Sam shook his head, "Again. I don't know who that is." He sensed the man spoke the truth. Something told him the man wouldn't attack him if he set him free.

"I'll set you free on two conditions."

"Yes! Please what do you want?"

"Promise you won't attack me."

The man nodded, "Attack you? Why would I attack you?"

"And two, you cannot tell anyone of this room," Sam watched the man's eyes to see if he could trust him.

"Listen. You have my word on both. I just need to check on Sabrina."

Sam took a deep breath and began untying the man. He hoped the man would go away and Sam would clear the room today. He didn't know how he would do it, but he knew he must get it done.

The man shook Sam's hand, "You have my word. Now, where am I?"

"Cecil Hotel, basement."

"Thank you," and with that the man took off and out of sight.

Sam's world spun upside down. He tried to make a list of people he could call for help, but they would all ask too many questions. He secured the room and looked up the nearest U-Haul. He'd get everything out of the room and moved somewhere else in the hotel, then figure out where to put it permanently.

———————

Jason Jang sprinted out of the room, down the hallway, and found the stairwell. He smashed through the door, up the stairs, and cautiously worked his way to Sabrina's room. Gun drawn, he made entry, and worked the room looking for

Sabrina. He did not locate her. His heart sank. Not only had he been hired to protect her, they'd fallen madly in love. Jason paced cursing himself for getting choked out. *I need to find her.* He searched the room for clues. There were no signs of a struggle, no note, and her cell phone sat on the counter. *Whoever grabbed her is very good...and knows who she is. I need to advise the consulate.* Although extremely embarrassed and genuinely concerned for Sabrina's welfare, he had to alert the higher-ups. They'd deal with his mistake soon enough, but they had access to resources he needed. *I'm so sorry baby, hold on. I will find you.*

Chapter Fourteen:

The work cell phone beeped alerting Peter that the contract had begun. He retrieved the phone, it scanned his face and unlocked, then he opened the Signal app.

"We reached out. They will pay. We demanded 5M. Proof of life has been requested."

Peter grunted, *damn it, I forgot to send her photo.* He began to think he did very little to collect a quick million dollars. *This seemed almost too easy.*

He downed the remaining bit of his Corona beer, pulled the book on the shelf releasing the locking mechanism to gain access to the safe-room and walked inside. He carefully lifted the black bag and jumped once he could see the woman's face. *Son-of-a-bitch! That isn't Sabrina Ma! Who the hell is that?* A tightness crushed his chest and he stared at the bewildered woman in complete disarray. *We just lost a million dollars. I need to text back a photo. What am I going to do?* The woman stared at him but didn't make a sound. It seemed like the girl studied him. It made him uncomfortable, so he looked away. He'd never messed up a job before and did not like how it made him feel.

"Negative. I have the wrong girl." He hit send with a pit in his stomach unlike anything he'd ever felt before. He reached for his own cell phone.

"I fucked up. It's no good. C U when I C U." Again, the pit n his stomach made him nauseous. *I can't believe I grabbed the wrong woman.* The error cost him five-hundred-thousand-dollars. Peter would not recover from it.

He turned to the scared and disoriented woman, "So, I bet you have a lot of questions."

The woman nodded, "Well, here's the deal. You don't get to ask any," he grabbed a black hood and moved toward her. She began shaking uncontrollably, "Relax. I'm letting you go, but I can't just open the door and set you free."

The girl nodded as though she understood.

Peter slipped the bag over the girl's head, escorted her out of his safe-room, and checked the hallway before taking her downstairs. He'd been so pre-occupied with his massive mistake that he didn't consider what threats might be lying in wait for him. He should have assumed the hotel would be crawling with cops. And, he had no idea Sam had freed the woman's bodyguard. Mistake after mistake lead to disaster.

"I'm going to take the tape off your wrists. I want you to count to one thousand before coming out. Do you understand?"

The woman nodded.

Peter removed the tape but left the woman's head covered.

"Who…who are you?" she asked in a shaken tone.

"An idiot," he shut the door and worked his way back to his room. *I need to disappear. Man, if dad were here, he'd be so mad at me. How could I be that stupid?*

Jason sprinted back toward the man that rescued him hoping he might have some idea about who would have taken Sabrina. The thought came from desperation. He felt helpless and ashamed for not protecting Sabrina. He got down to where he thought he'd exited before and couldn't find a door. *I know I came out somewhere down here.* He didn't know what to do next. *The lobby. They must have cameras.* He looked over his shoulder and saw a camera in the upper corner of the ceiling. *There!*

At the same time he noticed the surveillance camera, a man appeared at the other end of the hall that looked a lot like the man he'd fought. They locked eyes, and both instantly perceived the other as a serious threat.

"Hey!" Jason yelled as the man broke off in a full sprint downstairs toward the street.

From the surveillance they'd conducted, Peter recognized the man as the bodyguard. *Shit!* He took off running for his life.

Jason chased after Peter and clearly gained on him. They ran across the street, down 8th Avenue, and Peter used an alley hoping to avoid his pursuer. He looked back and didn't see anyone but kept running to a stash car a few blocks away.

Out of the corner of his eye he saw a dark flash coming from his right. He tried to duck, but the man bear-tackled him and they both ended up thrashing about in the alleyway. Peter tried to fight his way free, but the bodyguard countered everything he threw at him.

Jason finally got his arms around Peter and choked him as Thomas had done to him. "Where is she?"

"I don't know. We grabbed the wrong girl!" He had no idea why the man tried to kill him after he'd grabbed the wrong girl. *Think! Try to get away!*

"Where is she!" Jason squeezed harder choking Peter almost completely out.

"We grabbed the wrong girl. I don't know where Sabrina is!" he struggled to speak losing more air by the second.

At the mention of Sabrina's name, Jason relaxed his grip a bit. It provided the opening Peter needed.

During the struggle and pause, Peter had managed to get his hand on his pocket-knife and his right arm from underneath his own weight. With the little energy he had left, he rolled over and stabbed Jason in the arm. Jason had questions, but the pain radiated down his back indicating he needed to react swiftly. There wouldn't be any time for questions. *I'm not failing again. I need to find Sabrina.* With unbelievable quickness, Jason pulled the man's knife from his shoulder and stabbed the man in the neck. Blood squirted from the gash and covered Jason and Peter. He didn't dare let his grip go and he drove the knife deeper into Peter's jugular vein. Jason had killed before and knew the man in his arms would be dead in seconds. He moved himself away from the man and turned his focus to finding Sabrina. *I killed the only lead! This can't get any worse.*

"Jason?" he recognized the voice and spun around to see Sabrina standing there. She wore a jogging suit and covered in sweat. The look on her face pained him. She took a few steps back unsure of what she just witnessed.

"Sabrina?" He looked at the man he'd just killed, "They tried to take you." What had happened earlier, and just now, made no sense to him. The fact Sabrina stood before him confirmed he had not failed. An echo of police sirens filled the air.

"Take me?"

"Yes. He said your name. There were two of them."

"I waited for you and when you didn't show, I went for a jog. I found a great place to eat then came back. I figured you slept in." She knew Jason trained to kill and had been hired to protect her but seeing a man with a knife in his neck laying in his own blood didn't compute. Her thoughts worked to sort things out. The sheer anger on Jason's face had been something else she'd never seen before. Sirens grew louder and louder.

"Get your hands up!"

Three police officers bunched up on the corner of an adjacent building had their rifles trained on Jason. More police cars flooded the area. Jason put his hands in the air. He knew not to say a word. Without the details, the police would assume he'd killed a man in cold blood. He knew they'd be stressed, and he would do everything they said to survive. The sight of Sabrina, even though she still looked at him oddly, made him feel whole again. The love he had for her couldn't be explained in words, and he planned to propose to her once things settled down.

SWAT officers carefully approached and handcuffed Jason. They took him to Central Division for questioning. Sabrina returned to her room to find two more bodyguards. *I guess dad thinks someone grabbed me.* She checked in with her parents. She told them how she ditched Jason to jog and eat downtown. Her father despised her decision, but fortunate that his only daughter had not been taken from him. Her parents ordered her to return immediately. FBI and US Marshal's agents conducted a quick investigation, verified her story as well as Jason's, and escorted them to the airport. The Los Angeles Police Department requested Jason stay until they completed their full investigation. He waved goodbye to Sabrina having no idea that he would never see her again.

Chapter Fifteen:

January 28, 2013. Elisa Lam, aged 21, entered the hotel and asked for a communal room – a suite-like set-up that she shared with five other guests. Two days later, her roommates complained saying Elisa exhibited odd behavior. Hotel staff then provided her a room of her own. Those who knew her during the time she lived in the hotel described her as polite and out-going.

Medications she'd been taking had distorted her mind. She stopped taking two of the medications which became a critical mistake and caused her to think much differently. In the past, she had considered ending her life, but nothing super serious. Now the unbalanced medications unknowingly pushed her toward suicidal thoughts once again. Elisa, determined to end her life, opened her door and broke into a full sprint toward a window at the end of the hall. As she got closer, someone grabbed her from behind and picked her up off the floor. She clawed and scratched at the man while screaming. He cupped his hand over her mouth and she bit him. The attacker screamed in pain but did not let her go. He carried her and covered her mouth while running downstairs. *Let me go! Let me go!*

She didn't know where he'd taken her, but they went into a dark room. Elisa tried to make sense of what just occurred. *What is going on? Why won't he let me go? What is he going to do with me?* Her thoughts of suicide turned to wanting desperately to survive. *I need to get out of here!* Her hands and legs were bound to something hard, she assumed a chair, and her head had been covered with something. *Think Elisa, think. There's gotta be a way out.* She resorted to her ears and nose trying to see if she could pick up anything useful. Her heart rate finally began to slow, and she felt marginally better given the predicament she found herself in. With each minute that passed, and no opportunity for escape, Elisa could feel depression sinking her.

Suddenly, the man appeared. He removed the hood and spoke to her. She didn't know what to do or how to act but managed to nod.

He told her he planned to let her go, but she didn't believe him. He escorted her downstairs. He told her he would free her wrists, and she needed to count to one-thousand before she left.

As soon as he took the tape off her mouth, she asked him his identity. He did not answer and looked quite upset.

Then, as quickly as he'd grabbed her, he left, and she was free again.

She counted to one thousand then cautiously uncovered her face and left the room dazed and unsure of her next move. After a few minutes, she located the front lobby and thought about telling staff what she'd just been through. For some reason, she told no one what happened and retreated to her room. She didn't come out for one full day trying to comprehend everything and find the courage to move on.

January 31, 2013. David and Yinna Lam, Elisa's parents, contacted the Los Angeles Police Department to report their daughter missing. They hadn't heard from her for a day and assumed she'd be in Santa Cruz by then. While on her trip, she called them every day and posted online on her blog (named "Ether Fields") her daily activities. The last they knew, according to what they told the police, Elisa had been staying at the Cecil Hotel in Los Angeles. They would never hear from Elisa again. Police responded and searched her room, but nothing of note would be located.

February 11, 2013. Mr. and Mrs. Baugh checked into the Cecil Hotel visiting from Great Britain. They found the room suitable, but the hotel water caused them concern. The pressure seemed very low, it had an odd smell and taste, and when they turned on the faucet, the water came out dark brown. It would clear up within a few minutes, but they were not accustomed to water looking or smelling like this. For eight days, they drank and bathed in the water assuming the water would be the same at all hotels in Los Angeles' Skid Row.

February 19, 2013. Sabina Baugh decided to make a formal complaint. Staff had heard of the issue several times previously and did not act upon the information. Complaints had poured in for two weeks. After Sabina's complaint, a maintenance worker responded to the roof to check four tanks holding the hotel's water supply.

The first tank checked clear. The second tank contained a naked human body floating on the surface -Elisa Lam had finally been located. News quickly spread of the gruesome discovery and LAPD detectives were dispatched to piece together what happened to Ms. Lam. Almost immediately conspiracy theories spun out of control as to what happened to Elisa. A video of her final moments in the hotel would be released showing Elisa behaving bizarrely in a Cecil elevator. The video went viral, but it also added further confusion and speculation in the case.

After securing the rooftop, detectives worked with the coroner to process the scene. In the beginning, no obvious signs of trauma were evident, so police weren't sure if they were investigating a suicide or murder. They noticed the public and guests of the hotel could not reach rooftop access. There are two locked doors to prevent anyone from poking around. These doors are armed and send an alarm to lobby staff if opened. A proper keycode and another door is required to gain access to the alarmed doors. The maintenance worker defeated all these measures when he went to explore the complaint. The rooftop tanks are old with heavy lids, and based on the slight size of the victim, many thought someone had to be with her or put her in the tank then replace the lid back on top. Detectives questioned how she could have got herself in the tank and replaced the lid while inside the tank. Detectives also spotted a fire escape that led to the roof that anyone could have accessed to bypass the doors within the Cecil. More questions than answers developed initially with this case.

They drained the tank of water, recovered her body, and transported her to get an autopsy. Her Cecil room key, watch, and clothing were also located in the tank. A fine sand particulate would be located on some of her clothing, but no one had any idea what it meant or where it had come from.

Beyond speculation, police had very little to work with at the scene. They hoped the results from autopsy would shed some light on the case. While they waited, they released the odd elevator video of Elisa. They'd searched hundreds of hours of video looking for a clue and were left with her behavior in the elevator and one other lead. The video dramatically increased calls to the police department. Some find the video difficult to watch, but one can see Elisa pushing all the buttons, waving her arms, speaking, rocking in place, stepping in and out of the elevator car, and standing in the corner of the elevator. It does appear she's trying to hide, but from what we will never know. No other person or thing is seen in the video. Although she pressed numerous buttons, the doors did not close, and the elevator didn't move, forcing Elisa to exit it and move on. Several times it appears she's communicating with someone or something. Without knowing more, it's easy to see how people speculated and conjured up their own assessment for what possibly happened to Elisa.

The other lead developed through countless hours of video watched by the police. It appears two men meet up with Elisa and pass her a black box, medium size. The two men linger briefly in the lobby then exit. These men were never identified. In addition, the detectives followed Elisa via hotel cameras while she held the box and see her enter her room with it. None of the times staff or police searched her room revealed the box. To this day, no one knows what the box contained.

Police leaned more toward an accidental death but continued to rigorously investigate. They located her blog and noticed she often posted her struggles with depression and mental illness. Further, they learned she used this quote, "You're always haunted by the idea you're wasting your life," from Chuck Palahniuk, as an epigraph on her blog. Some suggested a super natural entity killed Elisa, others argued that she had been murdered. The autopsy report came out four months after Elisa's remains were located. Investigators learned Ms. Lam had been diagnosed as bi-polar and prescribed various medications. They assumed she'd become manic and her actions in the elevator video were a result of an adverse reaction to medications. The detectives discovered that patients could have many sorts of reactions to medications, including wanting to harm themselves.

Four different psychiatric medications used to treat bi-polar individuals were present, albeit some faint, at the time of the autopsy. The report listed: Wellbutrin, Seroquel, Lamictal, and Effexor. Often an anti-depressant is used in conjunction with a mood stabilizer and anti-psychotic drugs to manage the symptoms of those diagnosed as bipolar. In Elisa's case, it appeared she had not recently taken her anti-psychotic medications. These medications were meant to balance her, and since she didn't take them, it's likely the anti-depressants caused her to go manic. Manic episodes cause paranoia, delusions, and hallucinations. The way Elisa acted on the elevator certainly fit these categories. Officially, the autopsy report listed the cause of death as accidental and mentioned "Bi-polar" as a contributing factor to her death.

The autopsy should have marked the end of Elisa's case, but it did not. Since the results were not immediately released, and some speculated the police were intentionally hiding pertinent facts, speculation of how she passed continued to grow. Self-proclaimed video experts on the internet claimed the video released of Elisa had been doctored and over a minute of the video had been erased. Some people went as far as to suggest Elisa died while playing "the elevator game," an urban legend believed to take those who play the game to another dimension.

Books, articles, documentaries, and podcasts have been dedicated to Elisa's story. There is a growing number of people who believe someone murdered her and feel they have uncovered evidence to support that opinion. However, there just isn't any concrete tangible evidence that someone did in fact kill Elisa. Several detectives were assigned her case, none of whom believe she was murdered. The case could be made that we will never know for certain how exactly Elisa's last hours unfolded, but she should be allowed to rest in peace.

Chapter Sixteen:

Sam frantically grabbed items off the walls, careful not to rip them, and tossed them into cardboard boxes. Every second in the room scared him. The last few days made no sense to him and he didn't have time to figure things out. At some point he'd make sense of it all, but not today. He had a small pocket-knife to use for defense in case someone caught him in the room. Within an hour, he'd filled twenty-seven large cardboard boxes with nearly one-hundred years of work. Three or four at a time, Sam wheeled them with a dolly to the loading dock area. Once he stacked them all, he threw a blue tarp over them. Only one other co-worker used the loading dock leading him to believe the stash would be fine until further arrangements could be made. After most staff left for the night, he backed in a U-Haul, filled it, and transported the boxes to a 24-hour storage facility. Sweat dripped from his brow after he snapped shut a lock on the roll up door. *Ok, now what?* He hadn't thought things much further ahead than this, but moving the boxes made him feel much better.

Thomas knew the fact his brother hadn't responded to his texts meant something bad had happened. He couldn't recall his brother ever making such an egregious mistake, but the money didn't matter now. He felt in his heart that his brother needed his help.

He phoned him again and left a message, "Bro. Please call me back."

His phone vibrated, "911. Call me." The message came from a close friend residing at the Cecil.

Thomas called the man, "It's Peter isn't it?"

"Yes," a long pause followed, "He's dead."

"Dead! What? Where are you? Who killed him? When did it happen?" Thomas felt blood pumping throughout his veins at an alarming rate. His high blood pressure sparked his short fuse. The news of his brother being dead didn't completely sink in. He saw red and vowed to kill whoever murdered Peter.

"You need to calm down. Some guy stabbed him outside the hotel."

"When? What did he look like?" He imagined finding and killing the man over and over until the sorrow he felt began to numb him.

"It just happened. The guy's Asian."

The statement made Thomas pause, "Asian?"

"Yes. In a suit. The police took him away."

"Son-of-a-bitch!"

"What?"

Thomas assumed the bodyguard he fought with earlier killed Peter. *I should have killed him! How did he get free so fast? How'd he find and kill Peter? How the hell am I going to get him if the police have him?*

"Did the guy have shoulder length black hair?"

"Yes."

"Damn it!" The long hair, suit, and being of Asian descent convinced Thomas that the bodyguard had killed Peter. Revenge became the only thing that mattered to him. *I will kill whoever did this.*

Thomas used every connection he had to get intelligence on the bodyguard. He learned the man had been released by police after a few hours of questioning, a fact that only made him more upset because it meant he would likely get away with murder. He saw a woman with the bodyguard, who he assumed to be the original target, and he assumed her family would want her home. He chose a vantage point overlooking the international terminal at LAX. Since the man had seen his face, he chose to wear a disguise and a suit Peter had gotten him a few years ago. It didn't fit right, but it made him feel closer to his brother.

Two hours after his wait began, Thomas saw the bodyguard. His heart skipped a beat. *I'm going to kill you.*

Several other men and Sabrina Ma were with him. They worked their way to the terminal and inside. Thomas followed closely but with enough distance to make a quick escape. Everyone except the bodyguard got on the plane. *Why isn't he going?* He worked himself into a position to tail him back to his car. He followed the man downtown where he parked in a structure and left on foot. Thomas tailed him to a restaurant, exited, and followed to confirm he went inside. A waiter poured tea and Thomas walked quickly to the man's car. Before he reached it, he stopped by his own to grab explosives.

He looked around one last time before diving to the ground and rolling under the bodyguard's vehicle. Thomas worked fast to install enough explosives to disintegrate the car and the man who took Peter from him forever. Images of a lifetime with Peter, both as kids growing up and jobs they'd done together, danced in his head making installation difficult but with more purpose. After affixing the remote trigger, he rolled over, pushed himself and dusted himself off. The bodyguard returned, entered his car, and hopped on the ten to the five. Thomas followed waiting for a good place to dial the cell phone trigger. He wanted the man to suffer.

The bodyguard cleared the downtown area and traffic opened the further south he drove on the five. Thomas sped up to get in line with the bodyguard and got his attention. The guard saw Thomas and immediately swerved trying to hit him. Thomas dodged him, laughed, and saw the sign for the Disneyland exit. The guard turned hard right toward the Disneyland hoping surface streets would make it easier to elude Thomas.

Thomas yelled, "This is for you, Peter!" and hit send on the phone detonating the bomb. *I bet it's not the happiest place on Earth for you, asshole!* Body and car parts scattered across the interstate. It wouldn't bring Peter back, but it quelled the demons within for a moment.

Thomas made his way back downtown then caught a flight to Chicago with every intention of picking up the pieces of his life and starting over. Unfortunately, seven days after landing in Chicago, federal agents caught him on a wiretap. He's now serving twenty-five to life in a federal prison. All he thinks about is his brother.

Sam suffered a stroke shortly after unloading the boxes in the storage unit that he'd rented for ninety-days. He did not survive the stroke, and no one knew anything about the storage unit or what it contained. Eventually, the unit sold at auction. The new owners discarded all of Sam's boxes eliminating all ties binding the Cecil Hotel to crimes and death.

In 2014, the Cecil became, "Stay on Main." Once again, investors hoped to erase the hotel's remarkable past. It remains to be seen what happens next. It's been years since there's been a jumper, murder, serial killer, or unexplainable death in the building. Anyone who knows anything about the Cecil knows whatever happens next -and something will surely happen- it will be noteworthy…perhaps even an event someone will write a book about someday. Whatever the case may be, the Cecil will endure.

<u>Photos:</u>

Los Angeles' Newest
Hotel

OPENS
TODAY
DEC. 20

The HOTEL CECIL

Main Street Between Sixth and Seventh
14 Stories Absolutely Fireproof

700 ROOMS

300 with detached bath	$1.50
200 with private toilet	2.00
200 with private bath	2.50

SPECIAL RATES BY THE MONTH

The Cecil is most modern in every detail of plan, construction, equipment and furnishing. Fourteen stories in height. It contains 700 guest rooms and public rooms exceptional in number and size.

The public rooms are distinguished

in their symmetry of proportions and great beauty of decoration. The guest rooms are equipped with every convenience for comfort and luxury. Convenient to railway and steamship terminals, local offices, theatres and usual transportation facilities.

W. B. HANNER, President

R. H. SCHOPS, Vice-President   CHAS. L. DIX, Secretary and Treasurer

First known advertisement for the Cecil Hotel, 1927.

Advertisement for rooms, 1928.

Hotel Cecil, 1950's.

Cecil lobby, late 1980's.

Cecil postcard, 1930's (Replica).

Elevators at the Cecil, 1980's.

Cecil signage, 2010.

Point of view from the roof of the Cecil, 2012.

Homeless outside the Cecil during the Great Depression,

1934.

Former Soldier Takes Own Life

His throat slashed, Louis D. Borden, 53 years of age, former sergeant in the Army Medical Corps, was found dead in a hotel room at 640 South Main street. Investigating officers, finding a razor by the body and farewell notes, reported Borden ended his own life because of ill health.

In one brief note he asked that Mrs. Edna Hasoner of P.O. Box 664, Edmonds, Wash., "sole beneficiary of the little that I leave," be notified.

Newspaper clipping for Louis D. Borden's passing,

1934.

Search for Man Ends in Finding Body at Hotel

Missing from his home at 912 Strand avenue, Manhattan Beach, since last Saturday, according to police, W. K. Norton, 46 years of age, was found dead in a hotel room at 640 South Main street yesterday morning. A number of capsules, believed to have contained poison, were given by police as evidence that Norton had ended his own life. The capsules, police said, were found in his vest pocket.

Norton had been dead, apparently, only a few hours when found by a maid. He registered at the hotel, according to police, last Saturday as James Willys of Chicago. Several checks made out to Mrs. M. C. Norton, found in his clothing, served to identify him as Norton, according to the police report.

W.K. Norton's newspaper clipping, 1931.

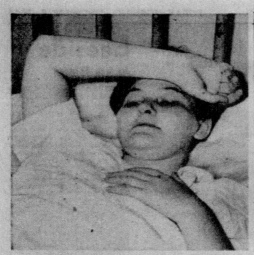

MURDER COMPLAINT—Dorothy Jean Purcell, 19, whom Coroner's jury recommended be held to answer on charge of throwing her newborn baby to his death from window of downtown hotel. She is in a hospital prison ward.

Mother Held After Baby Found Thrown to Death

After hearing testimony that one juror later described as "almost beyond belief," a coroner's jury yesterday recommended that Dorothy Jean Purcell, 19, be held to answer to a homicide charge for allegedly throwing her newborn baby boy to his death from a high window of a downtown hotel.

Miss Purcell, formerly a war-worker, was arrested Wednesday and held in the prison ward of General Hospital on a District Attorney's murder complaint after the baby's body was found on the roof of a building adjacent to the hotel at 640 S. Main St.

Testifying at the inquest, Police Officer Stewart Jones said the young woman had for several days occupied a hotel room with Ben Levine, 38, shoe salesman. She awakened, Jones quoted her as saying, early one morning to learn the baby was about to be born.

Not desiring to awaken her companion, the officer related, she went to the hotel rest room on the same floor and there delivered the baby alone. Believing the child dead, she threw it out the window and returned to the room, never telling Levine of the incident, according to testimony.

County Autopsy Surgeon Frank R. Webb, however, declared the baby was born alive, his lungs having filled with air.

Mother to Aid / of Her (

Mrs. Helen old Texas wit yesterday was sonal liberty af child neglect, by a court to county agencie four children proper homes.

Mrs. Crosley July 25 on su neglect after S investigated co home at 1704½ Her four childr more, 5, Janey, months old, we nile Hall after ert Ford, 19, while hitchhiki with the three released after his statement t had given hin take the childre Texas.

Justice of the lett, after read Probation Depu mendation that released and p tion for two her to 30 days Jail, suspended dered that as probation she the children fo

Mrs. Crosley mission to go was ordered to by mail. She h since her arres bail.

Child N

Trial Op

Charged wit three minor c care or food wh iting a soldier Barstow, Mrs. yesterday went a jury in Supe comb Condee's The three chil

WOMAN SUSPECT JAILED
IN CHILD STEALING CASE

Dorothy in the hospital awaiting trial, 1944.

Teacher Near Death

Miss Dorothy Sceiger, 45-year-old Riverside schoolteacher, last night was near death in the Georgia Street Receiving Hospital after having reportedly taken poison in her room in a hotel at 640 S. Main St., police reported.

pic Blvd. and W
was not held.
Urbano Royal
minguez Ave., V
in General Hos
received Dec. 1
struck by a car
Donatoni, 345 1
dro, at Anaheim
minguez Ave., W
natoni was not

Dorothy's blurb in the newspaper, 1940.

Suicide Kills Man

LOS ANGELES (UPI) — Mrs. Pauline Otton, 27, Los Angeles, wrote a suicide note to her husband then leaped nine stories from the Cecil Hotel.

George Giannini, 65, a transient, was struck by Mrs. Otton's hurtling body.

Coroner's deputies said both were dead at the scene Friday night.

Newspaper clipping for Mrs. Otton and Mr. Giannini,

1962.

'Pigeon' Goldie Is Slain In Her L. A. Hotel Room

LOS ANGELES (AP) — The coroner said yesterday that "Pigeon" Goldie Osgood, a 65-year-old woman familiar around Pershing Square, was strangled, raped and stabbed.

Mrs. Osgood's body was found in her downtown hotel room Thursday night.

An autopsy disclosed she had been choked to death with a hand towel, the coroner said.

Mrs. Osgood's trademark was the Dodger baseball cap she always wore as she fed the pigeons in Pershing Square. Packages of bird seed were found in her hotel room, where she had lived for six years.

Friends said they had seen her only minutes before her body was found. It was discovered by a man delivering new telephone directories.

Detectives said they are trying to determine if there was a connection between Mrs. Osgood's death and that of two other women slain downtown in the last two months.

A woman was stabbed to death May 16 in a hotel a block away from Mrs. Osgood's. Another woman, known for her care of birds in MacArthur Park, was stabbed to death April 29.

Goldie's newspaper article, 1964.

Continued from B1

up, surrounded the aging Hotel Cecil about 4:30 p.m. and quickly sealed all exits.

Reed faces trial next month in a drug-related gun attack on Skid Row that left one man dead and two adults and a child wounded, said Sgt. Tom Sears of the Sheriff's Department's Special Investigations Bureau.

Searching the hotel room by room, the officers eventually found Reed in Room 412, where he was arrested without incident, Sears said.

"He was standing in there with his back to us, his hands behind his head," Sears said. "He didn't say a thing. He seemed to know what we wanted."

Reed apparently flagged down a motorist Sunday morning near the Magic Mountain amusement park off the Golden State Freeway, said Deputy George Ducoulombier, a Sheriff's Department spokesman. Although wearing only his underwear and bleeding from razor-wire cuts, Reed told the driver that he had just been beaten and robbed. The driver dropped him off in central Los Angeles, the deputy said.

Deputies said the second captured inmate, 24-year-old Fernando Arroyo, was arrested about noon, dressed in a soiled T-shirt and light-blue underwear, after a construction worker in Santa Clarita called deputies when Arroyo asked to use a telephone. Arroyo later was spotted in a field across from the CHP station and taken into custody.

Meanwhile, more than 50 deputies scoured rugged terrain around the jail with helicopters, horses and bloodhounds as they continued to search for the two remaining escapees. But "as time progresses, there's a greater and greater chance they made it out of the area," Sheriff's Capt. Jeff Springs said.

The inmates still at large were

identified as Luis A. Galdames, 28, and Walter R. Padilla, 22.

Galdames, a Salvadoran gang member, was charged with fatally shooting one man in 1992 and another in 1994. Last month, he pleaded guilty to one count of manslaughter and to a handgun offense and was sentenced Thursday to 11 years in state prison. Padilla was sentenced Friday to seven years in state prison for a carjacking.

Sheriff's officials said they believe that the jailbreak was planned. "When you have 14 inmates involved in one escape, you probably have some communications taking place over several days," Ducoulombier said.

Deputies had patched the hole with a piece of sheet metal, securing it with screws. But inmates were able to remove the metal and escape into a heating duct where they removed another screen to gain access to the roof.

The escapees climbed the nearby 35-foot-high fence topped with razor wire, using bedsheets and jail uniforms to cover the wire and wearing socks as protective gloves. The escape was detected during a routine check of the jail grounds, when a deputy spotted several inmates scaling the fence.

Ducoulombier said an investigation is under way to determine the location of the lone deputy assigned to guard the 96 inmates when the escape occurred.

"There was some type of disturbance during that time frame," Ducoulombier said. "Whether or not it was a diversionary tactic we don't know."

The mass escape clearly un-

served some residents of the suburban enclaves around the jail.

Lisa Galvin, 40, who lives in a quiet development of Spanish-style homes known as North Bluffs, said she had not been fazed by previous escapes, which involved mostly minimum-security inmates. But on Sunday, she discovered two of the maximum-security escapees hiding under her BMW. They ran when she spotted them and were captured shortly thereafter.

Since then, she said, she has been carrying a handgun in the house, so "if they do come back I'm ready for them."

Another North Bluffs resident, Veronica Lopez, said she moved to the neighborhood from Palmdale with her husband and three young children three months ago.

"I thought it was better down here," she said. "I don't think I want to be here anymore. I think we'll be better away from jails, especially with kids."

A 35-year-old former aerospace worker who lives nearby said he was prepared for any escapee who might turn up on his doorstep.

"I've got my 12-gauge and my .357," said the man, who spoke from behind a screen door and would not give his name.

But other residents took the escape in stride.

"It's like what people say about California and the earthquake," Edie Baker said. "You still love it here."

Sheriff's Chief Mark Squiers, who is in charge of custody operations for the northern county, said officials plan to "remedy the weaknesses" in the 2,500-acre jail complex.

Squiers said inmates have been removed from the facility where the breakout occurred, the hole in the ceiling has been repaired and the area has been inspected for additional flaws. Officials are considering a number of other measures to boost security, including additional fencing, he said.

County supervisors last fall allocated $43 million to the Sheriff's Department to increase security patrols and to build a second fence around the maximum-security facility at Pitchess because of numerous escapes. But the low-security facility was recently closed because of budget constraints.

Authorities said inmates facing lengthy prison terms have little to lose by attempting to escape. Although an escape can add up to three years to a sentence, it usually adds only about eight months to a year because of credits for good behavior in prison, said David Demorian, head of the hard-core gang unit of the county district attorney's office.

Times staff writers Jack Cheevers and Eric Malnic and correspondent Mark Sabbatini contributed to this story.

Deputies capture escapee Fernando Arroyo in Santa Clarita.

Eric Reed prison break, 1995.

Richard Ramirez and Jack Unterweger, 1985/1992.

Richard Ramirez' arrest, 1985.

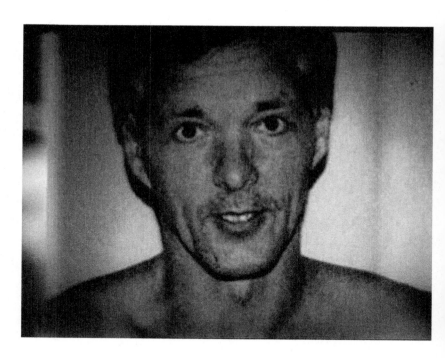

Jack Unterweger in custody, 1992.

Jack Unterweger working as a reporter, 1991.

Elisa Lam inside the Cecil, photo taken 2013.

First responders working to extract Elisa from the Cecil

water tank, 2013.

Disclaimer:

Reviews:

If you enjoyed this book, please leave a review on Amazon and Goodreads.

-Chris

Printed in Great Britain
by Amazon

56108182R00142